Me, Penelope

LISA JAHN-CLOUGH

HOUGHTON MIFFLIN HARCOURT COMPANY

BOSTON • NEW YORK

Library of Congress Cataloging-in-Publication Data
Jahn-Clough, Lisa.
  Me, Penelope / Lisa Jahn-Clough.
     p. cm.
  "Walter Lorraine books."
  Summary: Sixteen-year-old Penelope tries to find love, and to graduate from high school a year early, as she comes to terms with her little brother's death ten years before, and the resulting changes in her family.
  HC ISBN-13: 978-0-618-77366-4
  PA ISBN-13: 978-0-547-07632-4
  [1. Emotional problems—Fiction. 2. Guilt—Fiction. 3. Mothers and daughters—Fiction. 4. Interpersonal relations—Fiction. 5. Dating (Social customs)—Fiction. 6. High schools—Fiction. 7. Schools—Fiction.] I. Title.

PZ7.J153536Me 2007
[Fic]—dc22

                                        2006035626

Manufactured in the United States of America
HAD 10 9 8 7 6 5 4 3 2 1

Me, Penelope

I would like to thank the following fabulous people:

For wit, wisdom, and sustenance in various forms: Megan Boothby, Kirsten Cappy, Chris Demarest, Julia Ackerman, Stacy Graham, Liza Ketchum, Ron Koertge, Cathy Plourde, Whitney River.

For providing a room of my own in which to write when I needed it most: Pat Packard, Marion Wilson and the Lake Junaluska Writing Retreat.

For knowing (mostly) the difference between fact and fiction: Matt Spowart.

For reading early drafts with insightful honesty, for being an essential sounding board, and for true friendship: Ed Briant, Pam Richards.

For being my extraordinary editor: Walter Lorraine.

Me,

Penelope

Me

My name is Penelope Yeager, Lopi for short. I appear normal—normal for a sixteen-year-old American girl, that is. I live with a single mother who is still young and beautiful, more beautiful than I will ever be. My father left when I was six, after the accident. He moved across the country and I haven't seen him since. Viv says he has a new wife and two new children. He's moved on with a new life. I can't say I blame him.

Viv, my mother, has moved on by filling her life with activity and people, covering the memory with various substances, both legal and illegal, forcing herself by any means to be happy. I think she is in denial.

I have not moved on.

I look like nothing special. Longish brown hair, a smattering of freckles, thin lips that I wish were fuller, breasts a little larger than I'd like, hips a little narrow, but in general an okay body. I'm nothing to write home about, but

I'm nothing freakish either. If I put my hair up in a pony-tail I can pass for a lacrosse player, if I leave it stringy I can pass for a druggie, if I put it in pigtails and wear a baggy shirt I can pass for about twelve, and if I puff it up, wear a little makeup, and stick my chest out I can maybe pass for a college student. However, I am none of these things.

Anyway, it's not my looks or my body that dissatisfies me (most of the time)—it's my thinking. Mainly I can't stop thinking. Sometimes I want things so badly, all I can do is long for them until I get really, really sad.

I think that my mind must be different from others'. I don't know how people can be so together, so calm and happy all the time. I don't believe them. Take my mother, for instance. She appears happy, but how can she be, really? Her life has been full of tragedy. There are times when I am sitting there reading a book or studying for a math test, watching TV even, and my mind is off in a thousand places. Really what I am doing is trying not to think, but I can't help it. I think about the future, what I'd rather be doing, what could happen. I think about school and how things have shifted this year, how all I want to do is get out. I think about my friends and how I don't really have any anymore, except for Toad and that's changing— all we do is bicker like an old married couple, and we've never even been boyfriend and girlfriend.

Basically, I think about my life a lot, and sometimes to make my life better, I make things up. I think about how I want someone that I can talk to, really, really talk to. I'd like to see a shrink, but Viv says we can't afford one and that it's unnecessary for me, yet she sees one regularly. I saw one once when I was eight, but now Viv thinks I am doing fine. I am good at pretending.

And then there's sex. A lot of what I think about these days is sex. How to get it, if I want it, who I want it with. They say teenage boys are obsessed, but I think I have them beat hands down. Ha. Hands down, get it? See how my mind works? I have fantasy scenes going on a good part of the time in my head. If I could just find someone to connect with—really deeply connect with, the rest wouldn't matter so much. If I could only be touched all the way down to my soul, now that would be something.

Things I Want

1. To get out of this town, get out of the prison they call high school, get away from my crazy mother.

2. To have sex before I leave home.

3. To love someone. Really, really love him. Be able to say "I love you" a thousand times a day if I want without worrying that I am too much in love. (I don't know if number two and number three are simultaneously possible—somehow I doubt it. That's okay. I think I'd be too embarrassed to tell the person I loved that I was inexperienced, even though ideally it shouldn't matter. Ah, the hypocrisy of life.)

4. To get my driver's license, and not freak out every time I get in the driver's seat.

5. To stop thinking about what happened ten years ago. I was only six.

6. I want my mother to be happy. It may not seem like I want this, since sometimes I can't stand my mother, but if she were really, truly happy she might be more like the mother she used to be, and then maybe, just maybe, I could be happy too.

Escape from Prison

It is a warm, cloudless end-of-summer morning. I bike to the high school for my meeting. The meeting that will decide my future, my immediate future, anyway—who knows what effect it could have in the long run.

The idea is to get out of high school. High school is not for me. The rules, the structure, the grades. It's not that I am lazy or stupid. I don't want to sleep all day, like some kids I know. I happen to actually do better when I am in charge of my own time. I am a decent student; I just hate being in school. College has to be better. At least in college I can decide what I want to take and meet with teachers who actually care.

The cliques are what get to me in high school. There is a group for everyone: the jocks, the druggies, the nerds, the weirdos, the hippies, the intellectuals, the oversexed, the undersexed, the sexually confused, the band geeks, the art goths, the drama losers. There's even a group termed the nothings.

Sometime last year I figured I would either have to drop

out of school altogether or manage to escape a year early. If I have to stay in this prison any longer, who knows what I'd do. I'm not saying I'm one of those crazy, creepy kids who would blow up the school, but I can't say I haven't thought about it. I think every kid has that fantasy — or at least that the school will blow up spontaneously. There is a part of all teenagers that maybe, just maybe, understands that desire. Sometimes the only difference between good and evil is what we do with it. I figure the best thing is to get my sentence reduced.

Last year, I calculated that by the end of three years I'd have almost enough credits to graduate. The only class required all four years is English. If I took English over the summer I could take senior English this year.

I proposed this to the principal, Mrs. Miller, last spring. "It's possible," she'd said. "Take the summer class and come back before school starts and we'll see."

So I took Mrs. V.O.'s summer English class. It was mostly filled with students who had failed previously and needed to make it up, so she gave me a lot of outside assignments. It actually turned out to be great. I could read and write papers and work with her independently at my own pace. This is how I want learning to be. I don't want to sit in a class and listen to idiots.

It also gave me the perfect excuse not to have to hang out with Viv. Studying is the one excuse she will usually accept. She always wants me to do things with her, but then she ignores me. It's as if she needs me there so she isn't alone, but if someone better (i.e., a guy) comes along, she forgets me. I used to feel sorry for her so I hung out with her no matter what. But now I want my own life and my own friends. I want her to be okay, but I want to be okay too.

There are five adults in the principal's office when I arrive. Mrs. Miller, Mr. Oswald, the vice principal, Ms. Stein, the guidance counselor, Mrs. V.O., and Mr. Koch, the PE teacher. I don't know why Mr. Koch is there. He is the only one not seated.

Mrs. Miller waves me in and points to an empty wooden chair. "Please, have a seat, Penelope."

I feel as if I am on trial. Mrs. V.O. reaches over and pats my leg reassuringly.

Mr. Oswald looks at some paperwork on the desk. "So you want to graduate this year, Penelope." It's not a question, but it's not an answer either.

"I took English this summer," I say. "With Mrs. Van Orton." Mrs. V.O. smiles again. I explain my plan, even though I already explained it all at the end of last year. "I'll have all the requirements and enough credits," I add.

"I understand you did quite well this summer. Wrote some strong papers. Do you want to go on to study in English?" This from the guidance counselor, Ms. Stein, who as far as I can tell is mostly concerned with getting kids to stay in school and not get pregnant.

"Maybe," I say. "I like reading."

"Why do you want to graduate early?"

I was expecting this question and I am prepared. "I think I am ready to go to college. I work well on my own. And if for some reason I don't get in or don't get enough financial aid, well, then I'd like to travel abroad and work for a year to make enough money so I can go the next year and not be behind."

They all nod, except Mr. Koch, who has not said a word. I am still not sure why he is here.

"That all sounds logical to me," pipes Mrs. V.O. "Penelope is a very self-directed learner."

"There is one detail, Penelope, I am not sure you realized." This from Mrs. Miller. "You see, besides four years of English, we also require four years of physical education."

Finally Mr. Koch speaks. "We can't let you get away without taking all your PE credits." So this is why he is here.

"I think considering Penelope's academic record, her drive, her self-motivation, and her future plans, we could let the gym requirement slide." Mrs. V.O. is clearly in my corner.

"Physical health is just as important as intellectual health. I would think you, Mrs. Van Orton, of all people would be aware of that."

Mrs. V.O. is a big healthy living and sex education advocate. She runs the Lesbian, Gay, Bisexual, Transgender, Questioning, and Friends meetings (or LGBTQF). I don't know why they don't just call it the Everyone Club. Unfortunately LGBTQF is not a very popular organization in our school. This is a medium-size town, with only one high school of about 1,200 kids. No one wants to be outspoken, though I'm sure there are plenty of closeted LGBTQFs around. Our school follows the army's don't ask, don't tell code. It's okay if you are any of those things,

9

just don't go blabbing it. This is another thing I think will be better in college. More acceptance.

"I don't disagree, Mr. Koch," Mrs. V.O. says. "But these are extenuating circumstances. It hardly seems fair to make Penelope delay her plans of excelled study to take a year of PE. She's in good physical shape. Aren't you, Penelope?"

"I think so," I say. "I walk my dog. I ride my bike everywhere because I don't have my license."

"See? She incorporates physical health into her daily living. Just because it's not a competitive sport doesn't mean she's not in shape."

Mr. Koch is about to respond, but before he can speak Mrs. Miller says, "You were on the track team freshman year, weren't you, Penelope?" She checks the papers on her desk.

I nod. I was on the team for about a month. I went to two meets and hated standing around waiting to run, crowds gawking at us in the stands, and then having to race against someone else. I prefer my own pace and having Tessa with me, being outdoors, smelling the air in peace and quiet, with no gawkers.

I had not counted on the four-year gym requirement, however. This is a surprise to me. How had I overlooked this? I think fast.

"What if I agree to do some kind of exercise program, like running?" I propose. Mr. Koch's mouth turns downward. I continue. "It would be separate from gym. I'll document it too. Run every day, check my heart rate, do those government physical aptitude tests four times this year instead of two."

There is silence in the room as they ponder this.

Mrs. Miller responds first. "That sounds reasonable. Mr. Koch?"

All eyes turn to Mr. Koch. He knows he can't argue against all four adults. "I will expect a weekly report of your activities. Distances, pace, heart rate. You'll need some equipment, like a heart rate monitor, mileage counter. Can you provide those things?"

I say yes.

The rest of the group sighs with relief.

"You know you'll have to have Mrs. Van Orton again for senior AP English. It's the only one that fits in your schedule." The guidance counselor moves on to scheduling business, another of her favorites.

"Sure," I say. "That's fine."

Mrs. V.O. beams. I think I am one of the few students that actually like her. Others call her Mrs. B.O. because once she had pit stains under her arm. Kids can be so cruel.

"Okay, then, Penelope." Mrs. Miller prepares to close the meeting. She ruffles her papers, moves the penholder on her desk, puts down the pen she's been clicking the entire time. "We'll let your other teachers know—but basically the only class that you'll change is English. We'll list you as a senior so that you get all the appropriate materials and information to graduate at the end of this academic year."

11

"Providing the year goes well for you," chimes Mr. Oswald.

I fly out the front door, taking the steps two at a time. In one year I will be free! Free from this prison, free from Viv and all that goes with her, free to have my own life, whatever it may be.

When I get home Toad is sitting on the stoop with Tessa, my terrier mutt, who I got from the pound when I was twelve. Toad lives a few houses down and comes over whenever he wants. He helped me pick out Tessa, so in a sense we have shared custody, but she lives with me. She's really mine.

I grind my bike to a stop at Toad's feet. Tessa greets me with glee. I can't hide my grin of victory.

"They went for it?" Toad asks, knowing the answer. "Damn, you're good at convincing adults. Even with your geometry grade?"

Last year I got a C on my report card. Math has never been my strength. Everything else was A's.

"Nope, didn't even mention it. It's not being smart that matters," I say. "It's being clever, acting as though you have it all planned, so they can't say no. There is one stupid thing, though." I tell him about PE and Mr. Koch.

"That's Coach Cock for you. He loves his sports. I'm surprised he's not making you join some team."

"He knows I wouldn't be any great asset to anything. I suck at competition. I couldn't even handle the track team.

I have to build up to ten miles by the end of the school year."

"That's a lot," Toad says.

"I don't mind running if I can do it by myself. It'll be good for me. It'll be good for Tessa too." Tessa wags her tail happily. "I'll have to get a good jog bra, though." I clutch my breasts.

Toad turns red as he always does if anyone mentions anything related to sex or the human body. I jump up and give him a spontaneous hug. His eyes widen in surprise whenever I touch him. Sometimes I touch him just to freak him out, but this time it is from genuine joy. "One more year and I'll be out of here!" I shout.

Toad sighs.

"Aren't you happy for me, Toady-boy?"

"For you, sure. But I'm going to be left behind a whole year without you. I'll have to go through all that senior crap on my own."

"You'll be fine, Toad. You can handle it. I have great confidence in you."

Toad grunts. "Be sure to send me a postcard from paradise."

"Will do," I say. Today even Toad's sullenness can't bring me down.

Toad

Toad's real name is Harry Zebowski. He got the nickname Toad in kindergarten because he collected salamanders, newts, frogs, and any little bug that he could find in the swamp or under logs behind the school. At first the name was intended as an insult by the class bully, who called him a Hairy Toad. But after she moved the name stuck and Toad came to like it.

For a while we used to play fairy tale and I'd have to kiss him to see if he'd turn into a handsome prince. And then later he started calling me Frog and we decided we were best friends.

Even his teachers call him Toad. Most don't even call me Lopi.

Toad really is my best friend, though sometimes I love to hate him, and lately there's been something different about him, like something has come between us. I am afraid that Toad might be in love with me, and he's the last person I want to go out with. He's too good a friend to ruin it with romance. Romance never lasts.

Telling Viv

"They're going to let me graduate at the end of this year," I tell Viv and Tina as we finish supper. Ever since Tina moved in we've all been eating together at the table at least two or three nights a week. Tina is the college student who rents a room from us. In just three months Tina has become like part of the family. Viv is like that. She can become best friends with anyone instantly.

I like Tina. She is a senior at Concord College down the street, though she is older than the average senior, which is why she wants to live off-campus. I think she is close to thirty. She is definitely cool, in a relaxed way. I've never seen her wear anything but ripped jeans, and not the kind that are bought that way—she wears them out herself naturally. She doesn't care what people think of her, and it gives her an air that makes you want to know her. She keeps her hair in a pixie cut and has big eyes and a tiny button mouth. I'm pretty average and I feel like a giant around her. She also likes to cook, and she's good. She'll make a huge pot of stir-fry with pea pods, bamboo shoots, and little baby corn and add the perfect combination of spices, and whoever is around can have some. Sometimes Josh, Viv's new boyfriend (or BF as I like to call them), is there too, or one or two of Tina's friends. But not tonight. Tonight it's just the three of us. Tina has made an Indian dish with chicken, spinach, and cheese and puffed bread.

"Congrats, Lopi!" Tina says, raising her glass in a toast. "Graduating early — that's great! You're so smart."

Viv takes another helping of rice and vegetables. I wait, but she doesn't say anything.

Tina excuses herself to go study at the library. She tends to cook in the evening and then study all night. Tessa will hear her come in around two or three in the morning and give a quick bark to let me know someone is coming home before hopping back on my bed.

"Thanks for another great meal, Tina," Viv calls to her as she leaves.

Viv has still not reacted to my news. I'm not sure what her reaction will be. When I told her my plan last year she shrugged and said, "Go for it — if that's what you want." I don't think she believed I would actually follow through.

"The school needs final permission from you," I say. "You have to sign some form and go talk to the principal."

"So you will graduate high school this year?" she asks, as if it's just dawning on her.

"June fourteenth," I say. "Ten months away."

"They're going to let you?"

"I have to make up a PE requirement by running four times a week, and I'm taking senior English."

"You do study like a fiend." She smiles. "You never have time for your old mother anymore."

"You're not old," I say, because I know she expects me to. It's a routine we have.

"Of course not. But I am your mother. What are you going to do when you finish school? You can't just hang around here."

I tell her I want to apply to college, and that I've found a school that instead of giving grades requires student-initiated projects and papers. "I think it will be a good place for me," I say.

"No grades? Is it legitimate? Do they prepare you for a job?" Suddenly Viv is all curious about my future. "Is it expensive?"

"It's a good school. That famous filmmaker went there, the one who did that documentary on the history of jazz."

"Do you want to be a filmmaker?"

"I don't know. Maybe. I want to study where I can explore more of what I want. I want to do all sorts of things."

"We don't have money for school, you know. I was thinking you'd go to state or a community college, and not for another year or two at least. Study something practical, like nursing."

Like her, I think. *She wants me to be just like her.* Our house is full of stuff—paintings, pottery, sculpture, pillows, needlework made by Viv, but that's all just for hobby, a distraction, really, not something one could do for real. Not like a job. Viv is a nurse. She used to work

17

endless hours at the hospital, but for the last eight years she's been working part-time and gets disability for "psychological" reasons. So she says.

"There are scholarships and loans," I say. "I can work all summer too."

Viv grumps. "Yeah, well, you'll have to."

"So will you go to the school and sign that form?" I ask. "You need to do it this week so they can put me in the right English class."

Viv cradles my cheek with her hand and sighs. "My little girl all grown up and going to college. I'll miss you, you know."

"I know." For a second I think, *I'll miss you too.*

Viv takes her hand away and helps herself to more food. "I'm just grateful I'll have Josh around while you're gone. And now Tina too. Isn't she great the way she cooks? She's a find and a half. Maybe I can rent out your room to another student. Get some more income, fix up the place a little or buy a new car."

"Don't forget to go sign those forms," I sigh. "As soon as possible—tomorrow even."

New Clogs

The day my brother died my mother and I had gone shoe shopping, just the two of us. I desperately wanted a pair of clogs and finally convinced my mother that I would not trip in them. Now that I was six she conceded.

I tried on a pair of purple ones with yellow and pink flowers painted on the front. I clomped around the store. The salesclerk brought out another pair in my mother's size. Exactly the same—even with the flowers. My mother laughed, a fresh twinkle of a laugh, and tried them on. We both clomped.

She bought both pairs and we wore them out of the store—our old, ratty, unmatching shoes in the new clog boxes.

It was the first time my mother and I had ever gotten anything that matched.

We thunked and clunked across the parking lot. I hopped first on one foot then the other to make the sound louder, then skipped to the car to show my mother how coordinated I was in my new clogs.

On the way home we rolled down the windows, blared the radio, and sang to the wind.

This was something only my mother and I could share. I dreamed of matching print dresses, sun hats with large brims and wide ribbons flowing down our backs, and a world where my mother and father didn't fight and there was no baby brother in the way. Everyone would look at us and say, "There goes a mother and daughter who really love each other."

"You know what, pumpkin?" my mother shouted over the music and the wind. "It's such a beautiful day, let's see if the boys want to go to the beach for a picnic." The boys meant my father and the baby, Adam, who at two really wasn't so much a baby anymore.

"Can we wear our clogs?" I asked. I wanted to show off our matching clogs to everyone.

"Absolutely!" my mother said.

This is the best memory I have of being with my mother. By that evening our lives would never be the same.

First Run

I put on a pair of shorts, a sturdy bra, and a tank top. I lace up my sneakers, and head out the door. Tessa watches me eagerly as I do a couple of lame hamstring stretches on the steps and circle my arms in the air. That's good enough for a warm-up.

Tessa and I bound out the driveway toward the park. I have to cross a major road before getting there, but it's worth it. I stop at the curb and wait a ridiculous amount of time for a decent opening in the traffic. I won't cross until there is not a single car in sight. Tessa urges me on, but I tell her to wait. Finally my chance comes. I hold my breath and we both run as fast as possible to the other side.

The trail around the bay is just over four miles. Most of it goes along the water on one side with trees and green grass on the other. At one end is a playing field where various schools hold games and practices.

Today it looks like a game of soccer between elementary

schools. I remember those days. That's when playing sports was actually fun. It didn't matter so much about winning and losing, or letting the game define your personality. You could play soccer and play a musical instrument, be on the math team and in the school play. You could do everything all at the same time without being labeled. Was there more time back then? Or were we just more accepting?

Elementary school was so much better than now. It didn't seem so horrible that I'd once had a little brother—maybe I still thought he'd come back, I don't know. Maybe I just didn't remember what actually happened. Maybe I was in denial and one can only be happy when they pretend, like Viv. She pretends that she is happy, that everything is fine, so that I think she actually believes it.

There's a boy in my homeroom named Adam, and I can barely even look at him. It's as though even that name is tainted. He is never talked about at home; there's no picture of him anywhere. In fact, there are no photos of anything. Viv has filled the house with knickknacks she's collected and art she's made from all her adult ed classes, but no photographs.

I run for about ten minutes before I have to stop and walk. I didn't think it would be this hard. Tessa is doing fine, but she slows down with me. I do a run-walk the rest of the way. I count. Run for one hundred counts, walk for two hundred. Run one hundred, walk two. I check my pulse throughout—it stays about the same, but I am winded and sore. It takes more than an hour to do the whole loop. I'll have to start with lower standards. Maybe only two miles next time.

I write down my time and distance—exaggerating only a little bit. I don't want Coach Cock to think I'm not fit to graduate.

An Afternoon at the Beach

I am sitting in Algebra 2, staring out the window at a September sky of puffy cumulus clouds, daydreaming of being kissed. It's the perfect day to be lying on a grassy hillside with some lover. How I wish I had one. Someone who would lie down next to me, prop himself on his elbows, gaze into my eyes . . .

A girl knocks on the door and hands Mr. Hamilton a slip from the office. We all watch as he reads it. "Penelope Yeager," he says. "You are needed at the office." My daydream kiss dissolves. "Bring your stuff for early dismissal," Mr. Hamilton says as I get up. I think, *Thank god, anything to get out of this boring class*. I've never been a math fan, particularly when it's taught by Mr. Hamilton, who is far more enthusiastic about the football team than he is about equations.

When I get to the office, Viv is there. She is wearing a polka-dotted summer dress. Tendrils of dark hair poke out from under her sun hat.

"Lopi," she says. "You completely forgot your dentist

appointment. I just remembered for you when I saw it written on the calendar." She says this loudly, glancing at the secretary, who smiles at us from behind her computer.

I am about to say that I don't have a dentist appointment, but Viv keeps talking. "You remember, the last time you saw Dr. Roy he said he wanted to check those wisdom teeth again in a few months. Well, can you believe it's been a few months already? Time flies." She reaches for my hand. "Let's go. We don't want to be late."

I give a halfhearted wave to the secretary and she waves back.

"All right," I say once we're outside. "I don't have a dentist appointment. What's going on?"

"It's too gorgeous to be inside. We're kidnapping you." She points to the car. Josh is standing next to it.

He opens the back door. "Entrée, mademoiselle." Viv hired Josh last spring to paint the trim and he hasn't left, though he finished the trim ages ago. This is one of Viv's specialties—handymen. Josh is different, though. First off, he's young—much younger than Viv. Viv is almost forty, and Josh is at least ten years younger, maybe even more. He's a carpenter and a musician, never finished college, but he seems to really like Viv. Most of the time I try to avoid him, especially when I see him in the morning, dashing to the bathroom in his boxers, but he keeps trying to be friends with me. The daughter is the way to a mother's heart.

I climb into the back seat and buckle up. Tessa wags her

tail and gives me a happy lick. Josh grins as he closes me in. I take a deep breath. I hate cars, especially the Volvo. I am much happier riding my bike or walking, even running.

Josh opens the front for Viv, but not before kissing her. I turn away and pray that no one from school is watching.

"Do you know what today is?" Josh asks as we speed out of the lot. I catch his dark chocolate eyes in the rearview mirror—such a contrast with his sandy-colored hair. Will I have to get used to him? Or will he disappear like so many others?

"Thursday?" I say.

"No. Well, yes, it is. But it's also the first day of fall!"

"Fall!" Viv echoes. She rolls down the window. "Feel that clean, crisp air. Look at the colors in the trees." She sticks her head out and shouts, "Autumn!"

"Yahooooo!" Josh hollers. He starts singing, "Well, it's a marvelous night for a moondance," and Viv joins in. "'Neath the cover of October skies . . ."

"It's September," I say when they're done. "And it's daylight. And you should wear your seat belt." I direct this last comment to Viv.

"Oh, pooh." Viv turns around and frowns at me. "Would you rather we left you in that dark dungeon?"

She has a point.

Viv gives Josh a knowing look as though she can't do anything about me. She can't. Josh's hand is on her thigh. Do they think I don't notice? Do they think I don't care?

"Where are we going?" I ask.

"The beach!" they both exclaim at once.

I can't exactly protest. I love the beach. I am glad to be out of Horrible Hamilton's class. It is a gorgeous day. Warm. Sunny. Clear and crisp. One of those teasers where you think it is still summer. But it won't last: the days will get darker, the time will change, the cold will come. I will be shoveling snow in no time.

We stop at a store along the way and get sandwiches to go, then hop back in the car. This time I hum along very softly when Viv and Josh sing show tunes, burying my face in Tessa's scratchy black fur.

There are no cars in the parking lot, which is surprising for such a gorgeous day, but it is the middle of the day and most people have places to be, or they don't have mothers like mine who lie to their school to get them out.

We park near the snack bar, boarded up for the season. I let Tessa out and she immediately gallops off toward the water. We follow. You can hear the surf from the parking lot but can't see it until you walk through the dunes. Then the vast expanse of ocean opens up before your eyes. No matter how often I come to the beach, it never fails to take me by surprise. It's a breathtaking moment—that first glimpse of the sea. Today it is steel blue with peaks of whitecaps from the wind. I suck in the salty air. The wind has a nip, so I zip up my sweatshirt.

Josh runs after Tessa and they romp along the ocean's edge. He picks up a piece of driftwood and waves it over his head. Tessa jumps for it. Josh throws it in, and Tessa runs as far as the break line then backs up as the wave comes in. She loves the beach, but she won't go in, not even for driftwood. The stick comes in with the wave and she tries for it again, following it up to her ankles. The wave pulls it out and she follows until the water gets too close, then runs back to dry sand. She does this several times before finally managing to grab the stick. She runs down the beach with it, proud of herself. There is nothing more beautiful than Tessa running on the beach. She is so natural and free. Her mouth turns up in the wind and she is actually smiling.

Josh stumbles back to us, a little out of breath, and puts one arm around Viv and the other around me. "It is BEA-U-TIFUL!" he shouts.

Viv howls like a dog, then breaks away and starts running. Josh follows her but doesn't let go of my hand, so I have to run with him.

I think how utterly silly we must look—the three of us hollering and running like little kids. Well, I'm not hollering, but I am being dragged along. I pull back a little and Josh whispers in my ear, "Feel the wind, Lopi." He lets go of my hand and I keep running. The pounding of my heart matches the pounding of the surf. I am close to the edge and I can feel the spray in my face, taste the salt on my lips. I leave Viv and Josh far behind, but I don't care. It's the beach. It is meant for me. I forget everything: school, my life, Viv, Josh. Tessa runs with me, and we are both smiling. I hold my arms straight out and silent scream into the wind with my mouth wide open.

I run until my lungs hurt and then I fall onto the sand. Tessa circles me, digs a little hole, and collapses into it. I take off my shoes and burrow my feet in the sand. It's cold, damp, and grainy, but it feels great on my cooped-up feet. It's as if the world is made of only sun, water, and sand, and a few clouds and dune grasses. I wish I could stay here forever.

I wonder what the day would have been like ten years ago if we'd made it to the beach. Adam had been to the beach the summer before but was too young to really remember it. He loved the sandbox, though, and his orange pail and shovel. His favorite picture book was called *A Day at the Beach*. Ten years ago would have been his second beach trip, if it weren't for me.

I hear laughter and a scream. I sit up and see Viv and Josh in the distance. Josh is dangling a piece of seaweed over Viv, who is lying on her back. She reaches up and grabs his arm. He falls on top of her. They laugh and roll around, and suddenly go all quiet as they start to kiss.

I get up and walk farther down the beach. For all they care I could disappear. For all I care they could disappear. I find a spot in the dunes protected from the wind and lie in the sun. I wish I didn't feel this way. I don't care who Viv dates, and it's nicer to have her with a BF than not. When she's without one she wants me to do everything with her, and while sometimes that's fun, it's not so fun when she's complaining all the time about being single. I will never be like that. I will never need a man to make me happy. But then this thought makes me sad, because I don't exactly want to be alone all my life either. Without needing a man, how can I ever have sex? I just don't want to need someone all the time like she does.

I start to cry. I am seriously screwed up. Never happy, never satisfied. Never alone, never together. I want so much.

When I was young I thought I'd find a perfect friend. Someone I could tell everything to. It used to be my mother, in the old days, the good days, the before days. I told her all about school, who I liked and didn't like in my first grade class. We often did some craft project together or she'd help me paint the walls of my dollhouse. I loved watching her dress for work, sitting on her bed in the early morning. Everything white: white pants, white shirt and overcoat, even white socks and shoes. She'd put her hair up in a bun and tie it with a white ribbon. She looked like an angel as she told me stories about her patients and how she helped them. I thought how lucky they were to have her as their nurse.

After Adam was born, things changed. She would put him in his crib and then come snuggle in my bed, but inevitably he'd start to cry and she had to run over to him, leaving me to fall asleep on my own. He cried all the time. He was the neediest baby in the world. And his crying made my father yell more, which made my mother yell more, which made the baby cry more, until I just crawled under the dark of my bedcovers, my safe hole, and disappeared.

I imagined that my mother and I could have a life where it was just the two of us—no baby screaming, no father yelling. But that was a really long time ago. Now it *is* just the two of us and I can't remember the last time we ever really talked to each other. I don't have anything to say anymore.

Even Toad doesn't know the truth about what happened the day Adam was hit.

I think about disappearing in the dunes. I could copy Tessa and dig a hole, a really deep one, and crawl in. Cover myself with sand and suffocate in the grainy dark. When would Viv notice? Would she and Josh comb the beach, searching for me? Call the police? Send in a search team? Would she give up and go home and live a happy life? Sometimes I really think she would be happier without me—if she could truly start fresh, like my father did. I remind her too much of what she wants to forget.

Tessa comes over and pants in my face. I snuggle her snout. "I know you love me, Tessa," I say. "Don't worry. I won't leave you."

I stand up and scan the beach. I catch sight of two figures on the rocks at the end of the sandbar. At high tide those rocks become an island, but at low tide, like it is now, you can walk right out to them.

Tessa and I head over. Viv's white polka dots stand out against the gray rocks. I'm mad at myself for not having the willpower to disappear for longer, to let them wonder and worry.

They are eating sandwiches. "There you are, Lo," Viv says when I climb over the rocks. "Want your sandwich?"

I take it and sit behind them. I pick out a little piece of turkey and give it to Tessa.

"Beautiful day," Josh says. He touches Viv's arm. She smiles at him. I am embarrassed to be around.

"Having fun, Lopi?" he asks. His cheeks are red from the wind, and his hair is sticking straight up in a curly mass. He looks funny in a cute way.

I nod. "Sure."

"I bet it beats school."

I nod again.

"I would have given anything to have a mother as cool as Vivian." He beams at her. She beams back. *Spare me,* I think. They are like a Hallmark card.

We sit there until we're done with the food. "It's getting cold," I say. "And I have homework."

Viv sighs. "I guess we should head back then."

We walk back to the car slowly, even Tessa, as if all the running and wind have wiped us out. The drive home is quiet. Josh turns on the radio and I close my eyes and pretend to be asleep. Being in a car is better if I close my eyes and try not to think.

At night when I am in my room, ready for bed, Viv stands in the doorway. She never comes in anymore. "I hope you had fun today," she says.

"It was the best dentist appointment of my life."

Viv smiles. "It's important to me that you like Josh."

"I like him fine," I say, and then add, "Really. He's nice." I am not lying. Josh is nice.

"Good. Because I think—I hope—he just might be around for a while."

The New Book in Class

Mrs. V.O.'s class is the only class where there are no assigned seats. We can sit anywhere we want. The funny thing is that everyone always sits in the same seat anyway. Creatures of habit. Trained rats at seventeen. One of the American history teachers actually tosses out candy to anyone who gets the right answer.

I sit in the second row, two seats from the window. This is safe—not the first row like a brownnoser, not the back like a nodder (the ones who tend to nod off and subsequently always get the questions). English is my favorite class, so it does matter where I sit.

The class is all seniors. The only person I sort of know is a girl named Apple. She was in my art elective last year for about a week before she dropped it. She sits in the back row. Apple is one of the cool people. She can manage to get everyone to like her but doesn't need them to like her. She dyes her hair a new shade every month or so and dresses in a sort of hippie-meets-goth style that is all her own.

Today when we stream in everyone glances at the pile of thick paperbacks on Mrs. V.O.'s desk. There are two stacks, each with about ten books that reach at least two feet high. Mrs. V.O. grins gleefully as we pass.

When the final bell rings and everyone has slipped into his or her regular unassigned seat Mrs. V.O. starts passing out the books. "We are about to embark on a journey," she says.

The complaints begin. "It's sooooo long."

"Yes, it is long," agrees Mrs. V.O. "But good journeys take time."

"It's six hundred and thirty-six pages! And really small print!"

"You don't have to read the entire thing in one day, not even in one month. We're going to spend at least until break on this book. It's an American classic."

"Then why does the cover look like a trashy romance?"

I get my book and a smile from Mrs. V.O. The cover is frightfully dated. There is a square-jawed man lying in a golden cornfield in the lower corner. A red-haired woman in a faded red dress stands in the distance next to an old farmhouse. The wind is blowing her hair and dress, but the cornstalks are straight. Both characters look wistful. Across the type in a cloudless sky the title is written in cursive. *East of Eden,* by John Steinbeck. Mrs. V.O. must like him. She had us read a book by him last summer, called *The Red Pony*. It was okay. Much, much shorter.

"Is this a love story?" someone asks.

"Is it a Bible story? This doesn't look like the garden of Eden. Where are the waterfalls and the lush trees?"

"It's *east* of Eden, dummy."

Mrs. V.O. lets everyone get their complaints out and then says, "Before you get anymore bent out of shape, let me tell you that this is a timeless story. Sort of a love story, but really it's about family and good versus evil. What makes humans one way or the other? Or in some cases, with elements of both."

I hold the book as if it suddenly has weight beyond its bulk. Good and evil. This is my struggle. I stare at Mrs. V.O. Did she pick this book for me? I put the book down. I am almost afraid of it.

The Hole

The Hole is where I go. I don't know why I go there and I can't always predict when, but usually it's after a period of especially bad thoughts. I take myself out of this moment. I hide. I used to have to go to my room to do it, buried under my covers with darkness all around, but I've gotten so that I can do it in daylight, sitting up, in class, in the car, at the mall. Turn my mind off, think of something else, live in a fantasy moment instead. Sometimes it is a good fantasy, sometimes it is a bad fantasy.

Whenever I don't want to be here I go to my dark place, the place in my head that no one knows about. No one can see it or even guess it's there. The outside of me looks like a perfectly normal, good girl, but inside I am not good. I could even be evil.

The Hole can also make me feel better, because I can make things beautiful if I want. I can make it all work out perfectly, like a happy romantic comedy, or I can make it a sad, bleak tragedy.

Elwood the Shrink

I saw a therapist once when I was eight. I was having a series of nightmares and Viv thought a shrink would cure me. I sat in his rose-colored office in an overstuffed chair and we played games and then he showed me pictures and asked me to describe them. He didn't ask anything about my brother or my family. Then he called in my mother and told her I was perfectly normal considering what I'd gone through. So be it.

I liked him, though. His name was Elwood and he had a British accent and thick rectangular glasses. I thought he must be a great dad—that his kids were lucky to have a father who would smile at them and play games and tell them they were perfectly normal. (Even if it's not true.)

When we left the office my mother pulled my arm too tight and muttered, "A hundred bucks for that!"

Surprisingly the nightmares stopped—mostly. Now they only occur once in a blue moon, or very rarely during the day.

Ever since then, though, I've been talking to Elwood in

my head—trying to imagine the questions he might ask or the advice he would give. Not all the time like some crazy person, but just when I need someone to talk to.

I see myself, as I am now, sitting in the overstuffed chair in his office on a quiet, dead-end street. Elwood the Shrink sits in a wing-back chair that looks like it came from his grandmother. I carry on a session in my head.

"You know Viv's current BF is twenty-six?" I say.

Elwood the Shrink nods.

"Twenty-six! Isn't that crazy?" I say.

Elwood the Shrink keeps a poker face. I imagine that he is close to fifty now, maybe my father's age. He is sort of attractive in a European way. Skinny, sexy accent, clean smile. Why couldn't Viv go for someone like that instead of flakey younger guys? I've even made up for him an American wife and two daughters in college. He is the perfect dad, with the perfect family, which makes him the perfect shrink.

"That's almost fourteen years younger than Viv!" I tell him. "I'm only ten years younger than him. He could be *my* boyfriend!"

"Would you like him to be?" Elwood the Shrink cuts right to the chase.

I shrug. "Not really. I mean, he's cute, but it's gross the way he always kisses Viv." I wonder if I would ever want to kiss Josh, what it would be like to feel his dark eyes penetrating me as they do Viv, how his full lips and rough cheeks would feel against mine. "He is flirtatious by nature, though," I say.

Elwood the Shrink raises his brows. He wonders what

38

I am getting at. If there is something behind my words.

"I don't understand how Viv attracts so many men," I say.

"Why do you think?'

"I guess she's fun. She acts younger than her age. Men her age are too fuddy-duddy for her. When she was twenty-two she was with my father, who was fifteen years *older*. And *that* didn't work." I pause and think about it some more. "She always needs help too. And she asks for it."

"How do you mean?"

"Well, like, she can't do things because she's not feeling well, so she always gets men to help her. She acts like a child sometimes. I think men like that."

"And you? How do you fit into this?"

"I don't know," I say. "I mean, he should like me, right? I'm closer to his age. Does he think I am too ugly or too young?"

Elwood the Shrink doesn't say anything.

I go on, "I just can't ever attract anyone. No one is ever interested in me—they're all interested in Vivian. It's worse now. When I was twelve, thirteen, fourteen, even last year, twenty-six was still too old for me. I was too young and naïve. Now he's within my reach. Now I want to do other things. More things."

"Like what, Lopi?"

"You know."

He waits.

I sigh. "I don't want to go to college a . . . you know . . ."

He waits more.

"I want to sleep with someone," I say.

"Anyone in particular?"

"Well, no, not yet. But not just anyone, someone I love, obviously."

"There's a big difference between sex and love," he says.

"Yeah, I know. You think I don't know that? If my first time can't be with someone I love, then I'll just take someone I like for the experience. I don't want it to be a bad experience. How many people actually end up with the first person they sleep with anyway? It's just something to lead to the next one. Maybe the next one will be the one that lasts. Or not."

We both wait and then I say, "Kids in school have been doing it for years already! I'm like the last virgin on the planet!"

Elwood the Shrink adjusts his glasses and looks at me intently. He never tells me what to do, perhaps because I am only making him up and I don't know what I'd tell myself.

"I'd probably flirt with Josh if I'd met him on my own. And if he weren't screwing my mother. Maybe that's what I can't deal with. I have to see them together, being cuddly and kissy. Other people see them together and the same people always see me alone. I am always alone." I am on the verge of tears now. "Why can't life be simple? Why do I have to be so unwanted?"

In my perfect fantasy Elwood the Shrink tells me I am a beautiful young woman. In my not-so-perfect fantasy, Elwood the Shrink doesn't answer my questions. And sometimes in a really bad fantasy he tells me that it makes

40

sense that I am unlovable, that there is indeed evil inside me, just as I suspect.

According to the book we are reading in English, most people have bits of both good and evil in them, but sometimes there comes along a person who is all one or the other. In the book there is a woman who is so purely evil that she sets her own house on fire with her parents in it! Then later abandons her own children to start a brothel, where she steals from men. And wouldn't you know it— the one really good character falls in love with her and is blind to all her evilness. Love is blind, I guess.

Driving Lesson

Tina drives a tiny compact car, which is very suitable for her: she's so petite that she'd get lost in anything bigger.

She parks in the mall lot. It's Sunday morning and the mall isn't open for another two hours, so the lot is empty.

She gets out and walks in front of the car over to my side. "Your turn," she says, dangling the keys through the window. I stay put. "In order to drive the car, you have to sit in the driver's seat." She waves her hand. "We're not in England, you know."

It is Tina's big idea that she is going to teach me to drive, that I'll get my permit, then my license, and be able to drive myself to college. "You can't go to college without driving!" she exclaimed when she found out I had never been in the driver's seat. I haven't the heart to tell her that indeed I can go without driving. I get along quite well on my trusty bike, thank you very much. Besides, I plan to go to a school in a place where there is good public transportation and live in a city the rest of my life. A bicycle is more reliable, cheaper, easier to park, and safer than a car any day, not to mention better for the environment.

Tina was so eager to take me for a lesson this morning that I couldn't say no. However, getting in the driver's seat is another story. She dangles the key again and opens the door. "Scoot over."

I reluctantly climb over the gears and belt myself in. The seat is so far forward that my knees hit the dash. Tina reaches under my seat and tells me to push back. I find the right spot and she lets go. "Comfortable?" she asks.

I'm not comfortable at all. My hands are shaking, my heart is beating extra fast, the pavement in front of me begins to blur and merge into the same slate color as the highway beyond it and the sky above it.

Tina hands me the key. "This goes in the ignition. When you turn it, keep your foot on the brake. The brake is the pedal on the left. The other is the gas. Keep this shift here on P until you're ready to roll."

It sounds so simple. Everyone does it. Toad got his license the minute he could—he even drives a stick shift, saying automatics are for wusses. He bought himself an old Mustang a few months ago and treats it like a pet. I don't mind riding in his car as much as Viv's. Tina's little Escort shouldn't be so difficult. So why does it feel so complicated? The worst part is that everything starts to go foggy and blurry. I am not crying, but it's as if my eyes are full of water anyway, and my head is all muddled.

Keep it simple. This is easy, I repeat in my head. I take the key from Tina and do as she says. The engine hums on.

It's a quiet car, nothing like Toad's or Viv's. Viv got rid of her first Volvo after Adam but replaced it with the same kind, just a different color. Blue instead of silver. "I need the space to lug stuff around," she always says, "and I'll be damned if I get one of those idiot SUVs."

I will ride in the Volvo with Viv if there's no alternative, but I don't want to drive it, ever.

"Good," says Tina. "You got it." She is trying to encourage me. She knows I hate cars, but she doesn't know why. Only Viv and Toad know why. Viv has conveniently forgotten and Toad is nice enough not to ever mention it. Actually, I think he likes having me dependent on him for the occasional ride.

"The rest is easy," Tina says. She explains the gears. "P for park, D for drive, R for reverse, and N for neutral. The numbers are for upshifting but you almost never need to do that unless you're going up a really steep hill or you need more traction. Try backing out of the space. Be sure to check your mirrors."

I look in the rearview mirror. Nothing but the mall entrance is behind me, but it's all hazy like a mirage in a desert. I wipe my eyes to try to clear them. I put the shift to R and step on the gas pedal. Something flashes in the mirror, and a little boy with blond hair is standing behind the car, clear as day through the fog. I gasp. He is holding a plastic orange pail and shovel. He is all ready for the beach. His diaper bulges out of his yellow swimsuit, making his skinny arms and legs look even skinnier. He is grinning and waving frantically at me. I panic. I put my foot down hard. Too hard. The car jolts back really fast.

"Brake! Brake!" Tina screams. She pulls up on the emergency brake between us, and the car jerks to a stop. I find the foot brake. The boy in the mirror is gone.

"What happened?" Tina says.

"I . . . I . . . Something was behind me. I may have hit it." I don't tell her it was Adam.

"I didn't hear anything—the lot is empty." Just to be sure, or maybe to humor me, Tina gets out of the car and examines the back. I hold my breath as she bends down to look underneath. She gets back in. "Nothing there. You must be imagining things. Try again."

I look at her like she is crazy.

"You're never going to learn if you give up that easily. Take a deep breath. Try going forward."

This time I manage to take it slower. The car inches ahead. My hands are shaking but at least I can see that the pavement in front of me is empty.

I drive slowly around the lot, making a few wide turns. Seeing Adam appear like that is still making me shake—it's been a while since that's happened.

I was excited to go to the beach that day too. My mother and I had our new clogs. My father was driving. Viv was next to him. They started arguing about something, I don't know what, but their voices were loud and angry. I hated it when they argued. Adam started to cry. It was my job to strap Adam in his car seat, but he was struggling and wiggling too much, wailing about his pail and shovel. I didn't explain to him that his pail and shovel were in the back. Instead I gave up and he left the car, slipped right out the door and managed to close it behind him. I didn't stop him. I didn't tell my parents. I thought maybe they would notice and stop arguing, or that he'd get left behind and we could go to the beach without him. I didn't say anything. I didn't do anything. He went looking for his pail. I didn't think he'd look under the car.

Viv was yelling. My father started to back out of the driveway. They thought Adam was in his car seat, but he must have been crawling, crawling, crawling and so small and skinny that he was no more than a tree root in the path. The car backed up and there was a big bump, that awful sound, and then nothing.

"Lopi? Are you okay?" Tina is asking me. My breathing is fast and I am choking back tears; a few escape. I can't see anything through the blur.

"Maybe this is enough for today," she says.

I stop the car and hand the key over to her. She pats my back until I calm down. "Thanks for trying," I say.

My Friend Holly

When I was in first grade there was this girl named Holly. Holly was a terror. She threw tantrums when her mother dropped her off, she threw tantrums when her mother picked her up, she wet herself at least once a week, and she growled at everyone.

Holly carried a stuffed monkey around with her everywhere. It had long arms and legs with Velcro so she could attach it around her neck and let it drape over her shoulder. If anyone tried to touch her monkey she would scream. Once she even bit a kid. Everyone was afraid of her, and so we mostly ignored her and let her sit in the corner and stew. Even the teacher gave up after a while.

Holly's mother never stayed long enough for the teacher to talk to her. At drop-off Holly would cling to her mother, screaming she didn't want to go to school. Her mother had to peel her off and close the door so Holly couldn't get to her again. Once I saw the mother crying as she left. Holly would run to her cubby, yelling and screaming, and the teacher spent all morning calming her down.

When my mother dropped me off we just walked away from each other. I loved going to school.

For some reason Holly was nice to me. One day during recess she sat on the swing next to me and whispered, "I like you. Will you be my friend?"

I said yes because I was too scared to say no, and I was kind of honored that she chose me above everyone else.

From them on, every day she brought me a treat— a rock she had found on her way to school, an extra cookie. Her morning tantrums weren't quite as bad.

I asked her why she cried every time her mother dropped her off. She told me she loved her mother and never wanted to leave her. "But it's better now because I have you here," she said.

Holly is the only person I've ever told the truth about Adam. One day when we were supposed to be napping, I told her that I once had a brother but that I had killed him. She cried and hugged me and said, "That's so sad, but maybe he wanted to be dead."

One day she handed me her stuffed monkey. "You can have him," she said. "We're moving and he should stay here with you."

A week later she was gone. I never heard from her again, and I'm not sure where she went. I still have the monkey— he sits on the top of my dresser.

Playing with Fire

By early November the weather turns. It is a quiet, cold evening in the house. For once I am alone. Viv is at a movie with a friend and Tina is at the library. It's cold enough for a fire. I roll paper logs and throw some kindling in the fireplace to get a good flame roaring. I am cuddled up on the couch with some popcorn, Tessa at my side, and a book in my hand, when there is a knock at the door. It never fails. Just when I think I am going to have some alone time, I am interrupted.

Josh waves through the window and I let him in. Tessa jumps on him and does her happy-to-have-company dance.

"Hi," I say. "Viv's not here."

"That's okay," he says. "I was just driving by and figured I'd stop. Where is everyone?"

"Out. I'm the only one home. Enjoying the peace. Reading a book." I hold it up to prove it.

"*East of Eden*. Hmm. Must be hell."

I give him an annoyed look and throw a log on the fire, then sit down again. Tessa, realizing this company does not mean a walk, resumes her snuggle position.

"Just kidding," Josh says. "No need to be so touchy." He sits down next to Tessa and rubs her ears.

I guess he assumes he's invited to stay.

"No offense, Josh, but I was looking forward to this book."

"Go ahead, keep reading. I won't bother you. It's just nice to have company. My apartment is so empty sometimes."

There is something sad about Josh. I try to see what Viv sees in him. He is cute, with soft curly hair and a rough goatee. He sure loves to dance, and he is good at fixing things. Once I overheard him reading a poem out loud to her. It was sweet. But I feel sorry for him. Viv is sure to dump him at some point. Her boyfriends never stay long, though Josh has already made it almost six months, which is a record for Viv.

The few times Viv went out with someone older, usually someone she met through the personals or was set up with, she came home early and bored. She's too fast-paced for them. I'm the slow one. Our roles are completely reversed. I'll probably end up with someone twenty years older than I am, feeding him pills and changing his bedpan, while she will get some youthful, thriving lover to keep her active. I can't ever imagine Viv old or slowing down. Even my father went younger when he remarried. Is this what people need to do to make them feel better—always sleep with someone younger? Could it be, then, that my future lover is right now only five years old? Eww.

I try to concentrate on the book, but the words aren't registering. It's impossible for me to read with someone else sitting next to me. Josh sits in front of the fire and starts fiddling with the embers with the poker. I put the book down.

"What's the matter?" Josh asks.

"I can't read with you here."

"I'm not doing anything."

"You're making me nervous."

He comes back to the couch and slaps his hands on his lap. "Well, let's talk then."

I sigh. "About what?"

"Anything. Tell me about school."

"I'm just biding my time in that prison until I can go to college."

He laughs. He thinks I am kidding. "What about your friends?"

"What friends?"

"Surely you must have friends at school?"

"Some." I shrug. "They're all right." The first year of high school is like a trial year. If you pass, then you can stay in your group. If you don't pass, then you get demoted into one of the lesser groups. The whole group thing doesn't make sense to me. In fact, I think it's idiotic, which is why I was downgraded into no man's land. I am the type who doesn't have any group; I can almost sort of fit into a variety of groups if I really try, but I reject them

51

all by personal choice. So yeah, no one hates me; it's just that no one considers me in their group, so I am easily forgotten."

"A boyfriend?" Josh asks.

I hesitate a second, thinking how to answer. Finally I decide on the truth. "Not currently."

"Oh, come on!" He pushes my shoulder playfully. "There's got to be someone you have your eye on."

"The boys in high school are immature." It is true. They think they are all high and mighty because they do this or that, but even the seniors are lame.

"Come on, you can tell me. You must have a crush."

I look at him askew. A crush? Doesn't he know what people do in high school these days? Oral sex is all the rage. The whole basketball team brags about who gives the best head. I'm just relieved it isn't me. That's not exactly what I want my reputation to be, but that doesn't mean I haven't thought about it.

"You do, don't you?" Josh sidles up to me as if he has a secret. He is sweet in a puppy-dog kind of way. I am overcome with an urge to pat his head. I don't.

"Do what?" I ask, though I know what he means. Is he flirting with me? I sit up and smile. I can be flirty too.

"Have a crush."

"How do you know?" I ask.

"Because you deny it. Denial is the same as admission."

"Well. Maybe. Maybe not. But *crush* is not exactly a term I'd use."

"Oh, yeah? What term would you use, Miss Smarty-Pants?"

"Anything but *crush*. That is so juvenile. *Crush* implies that it'll never go anywhere or amount to anything."

"That's what makes it so much fun."

"Painful is more like it. A crush can never be real."

"Are you searching for something real, Lopi?"

I think before answering. "Of course. Who would want something fake?"

"You could just have fun, without being all serious. You're what, sixteen? You should be having fun!"

"Like Viv?" That gets him.

"Well, Vivian is fun. You can be fun and real at the same time."

"So then you have more than a crush on Viv?"

"I think so. Maybe. I'm enjoying myself. And so is she. And so should you." He brushes my arm with his hand and I pull back, but not before feeling a twinge of something kind of like excitement. I am surprised that I actually like him touching my arm. I wish I hadn't pulled away so fast.

Josh goes back to poking the embers, making them burst into orange flickering sparks. One of the logs lets out a loud snap, then crackles. I think about all the guys I know. Everyone else is doing it and all I can do is think about it.

The last time I kissed someone was at Stephanie Rosenthal's New Year's Eve party, freshman year. Parnell. We sat next to each other in art class all fall. He used to draw me little sketches of bulgy-eyed creatures resembling our various teachers and classmates. We had some great talks too. About art and life. Deep stuff.

After a while people started telling me we'd make a cute couple. That bugged me: I hadn't thought about him that way, and now I had to. People must have told him the same thing, because at Stephanie's party he came up to me with a bottle of champagne. He took a long swig and handed it to me. I took a swig and gave it back. I didn't think he would try anything since I'd heard he was pretty shy around girls, but when the clock struck midnight he grabbed me tight on the shoulders and kissed me hard, jamming his tongue into my mouth. I kissed back. I figured I might as well. I didn't get to kiss too often, and even then I wanted to get the experience. The kiss went on for an uncomfortably long and uncomfortably wet time. He tasted like cigarettes, which surprised me because I didn't think he'd be the type to smoke.

His tongue reminded me of those lamb's tongues you see in jars at the gourmet market. The long, meaty ones that are all squished together in congealed liquid. I wondered if our tongues would look the same if they were in a jar.

As he kissed me he put his hand down the back of my pants and rubbed my butt. When he finally stopped I sighed with relief and wiped my mouth and said something like "Blech." The lingering cigarette taste was so strong that I actually spit on the floor.

Ever since then things have been weird with Parnell. He stopped sitting next to me in art class—no more goofy drawings. Now he's quite the pot smoker. He's grown his hair long and dresses all goth. He's really gotten into the artsy stoner group, though he's too stoned to do much real art. It's a pretty fake act if you ask me. Maybe if I'd refused to kiss him we'd still be friends.

Does everything that has to do with sex always ruin things? This is why I have to have sex already and be done with it, move on to the good stuff, whatever that is. I do want sex, but sometimes I wonder if that is just my act. Because if I did really want it, wouldn't I have had it by now? Viv always tells me if you really want something you'll find a way to get it. She isn't talking about sex, exactly, but she may as well be.

"Hey! LO!" Josh snaps his fingers in my face. "I asked you a question."

"Huh?"

"Where is your mind?"

I can't tell Josh what I am thinking. I brush the hair from my eyes and sneak a glance at him. His mouth is in a wide grin, showing slightly crooked teeth, and his eyes make tiny creases in the corners. I imagine him coming over to me and saying something ridiculous like "You've got great tits," and then running his hands through my hair, down my neck and shoulders, where they would cup my breasts. He'd give me a long, passionate kiss, not like a lamb's tongue at all, because he knows how to kiss a girl. "Is this okay?" he'd whisper. I'd nod and suddenly he'd be on top of me, and clothes would come flying off. I'd unzip his pants . . .

Oh my god, my mind is full of it. I shudder.

"So are you going to tell me about your crush?" Josh asks.

I turn my face away, embarrassed by my thoughts. I glance back at him. He looks so thoughtful and sincere, so sweet and lovely, so manly and mature. He would know exactly what to do with me. Right then and there I realize that Josh is perfect.

"I don't have a crush on anyone," I say. "I'm looking for something better."

Apple

I decide to brave it and run on the official running path this time rather than along the road. Other runners call out, "On your right!" "Passing!" "Coming past!" and run by me. I don't care. Let them.

"Hey, I know you." One runner slows down. It is Apple from Mrs. V.O.'s class. She is wearing dark sweats with a fat white stripe down the sides and a nylon jacket unzipped to reveal her jog bra. Her hair is dyed wild red; her cheeks are bright. "You're in my English class," she says.

"Yeah."

She turns around and hop-jogs backwards as I walk. "I'm Apple. You're that junior who skipped, huh? I didn't know you were a runner."

"Have to," I say. Her face makes a question so I explain in short breaths that condense in the cold, "To graduate I need four years of PE. This is my makeup."

She makes a clucking sound with her tongue. "Wouldn't

you figure. This country is so sports obsessed. Fail any other class, but gym, oh my god, you'll never survive. Gym has a four-year requirement, but science doesn't? What about art? Creative people are more essential than athletes. And the irony is that so many people in America are overweight anyway!" She is done with her rant, I think. She's not even breathless. By this time we've both slowed down to almost a stop. She stoops to pet Tessa. "Hey there, funny-looking. What kind of dog is she?"

"Don't know. I found her at the pound."

She rubs Tessa and stands back up. "How much do you have to run for your requirement?"

"Four times a week. I have to document it—the goal is to get to ten miles by the end of the year."

"If you need someone to run with, let me know. Once you're able to keep up, that is."

"Okay," I say.

"Or if you want to go to a party sometime, I'm into that, and you seem cool. Anyone who's smart enough to get out of the hellhole they call high school has got to be okay."

"That'd be fun," I say. All this time I've been wondering how to be friends with someone like Apple, and I'd never thought running would do it. Who knew someone like her even ran?

"Okay, then. See you later. What's your name again? I know I know it, but I really suck at names. It's nothing personal."

"Lopi."

"That's right. See you later, Lopi."

She runs off around a bend of trees. Tessa runs after her for a second and then bounds back to me. I walk a bit more and then do a slow jog back home. I write my time and distance in my running log for Mr. Koch. Two miles in twenty-seven minutes.

Viv's Birthday

Viv has been planning her birthday party for months. Her birthday is more important than Christmas and New Year's combined and comes soon after.

"I'm going to celebrate with flair," Viv said when she sent out more than a hundred invitations. She didn't expect half of them to actually come. I think she just wanted to send announcements proving that she is still wild and crazy even though she is forty.

There's never been planning around my birthday, but that's no surprise. My birthday is in May and the last party Viv gave me was on my thirteenth. She had it at the local swimming pool. She took me there to go for a swim and thirty of my classmates, some of whom I barely even knew, greeted me as I left the locker room in a bathing suit so worn, it rode down my chest and up my butt in the most unattractive way ever. No, there'll be no more surprise parties from Viv to me.

But tonight is Viv's birthday and that is different. Viv is decked out in a fancy dress and boots and goes downstairs to do the last-minute preparations. I take a long hot shower and shave my legs. Afterward, I stand naked in the steamy bathroom and cover my body with almond oil. I squeeze droplets onto my shoulder then rub down the length of my arm. The almond smell intoxicates me as I oil my legs and admire my smooth shaving job. Someone will sure love to run his hands down those silky legs. And I know just the hands I want. Tonight is going to be the night. Viv won't notice since she'll be preoccupied with the party and all her friends. She might show Josh off for a few minutes, but then he'll have to hang out with me and I'll have him all to myself.

I put on my lace bra and matching panties. I had planned to wear my red velvet pants, but when I unfold them I notice a tear in the seam of the crotch. "Damn," I say, searching through the bathroom closet for a needle and thread.

I sit on the toilet seat and hurriedly sew up the seam.

"LOPI!" Viv calls from the top of the stairs. "What're you doing up there? People are arriving and I need your help."

"Down in a minute," I call back. I tear the thread with my teeth and tuck the end back into the seam so no one will notice. I stand up and check it out in the mirror. Good as new.

I try on about five tops before I decide on a cream-colored one with tiny buttons up the front. I put a dab of makeup on my eyes and lips, and smile. I fluff up my hair. I make a little ponytail on the top of my head like a whale spout and tie it with a silk scarf. I suck in my stomach and rub my hands down my body. I look good.

"LOPI!" Viv yells.

"Coming!"

There are about ten people downstairs already. Viv is using the dining room table as a buffet and is busy trying to arrange the food and greet everyone at the same time. It is a dessert party, a "bring your own" kind of thing. Viv, Tina, and I made tons of cookies and a cake earlier, which are now on plates in the center of the table. Already there looks to be plenty of food. And plenty of drinks. Viv has dragged in an old tin tub from the barn and filled it with ice and bottles of beer. A variety of wines and other kinds of liquor are lined up on the counter.

"It's about time," Viv hisses, shoving a pile of plates at me. "Put these out and make sure the table looks nice. I have to say hello to Sandra. I can't believe she came all the way from Connecticut!" She leaves me and goes screaming her way to the front door, where Sandra had just come in.

I watch them hug and kiss as though they haven't seen each other in years. Which is true. Sandra worked at the hospital until she married an insurance salesman and his three sons and moved to Connecticut almost two years ago.

I turn away from them and survey the wines. I pick a deep red one because it matches my pants and pour half a glass. Something to hold so I don't look like an idiot. No one will notice. I take a sip. It tastes a little acidic and burns as it goes down, but I like the warm feeling it leaves in my stomach. I gulp the rest. *I'm going to get drunk,* I think. *Especially if I'm going to go through with my plans.*

"Penelope, is that you?" Sandra is at my side. "Vivian, is this ravishing creature your daughter? You're a real woman, Lopi. How old are you now?"

"Sixteen."

"Gosh, a lot happens in two years at your age. Come here, give me a hug." Sandra is not a small woman. She engulfs me in a wave of arm and pulls me close. She smells of citrus.

"Did you bring your husband and the boys?" I ask when she lets go and I can breathe again.

"Nah. I need a vacation from the men. I love that guy, and the boys too, but sometimes there's just too much testosterone in that place." She puts her hands on my shoulders and squeezes. "I can't get over you, Lopi. Vivian, do you realize what a beauty your daughter is? She must have everyone drooling over her. Ah, to be sixteen again."

Viv eyes me. "What did you do to your hair?" she asks.

"Nothing," I say. I put the wineglass down.

"I can't believe you are forty and have a teenage daughter, Viv," Sandra says, filling the silence, or oblivious to it, I'm not sure which. "I don't know how you do it. If my body went through a pregnancy I'd never recover. So"— she puts her arm around Viv and scans the room—"is that cute young thing you've been raving about here?"

"Not yet," Viv says, suddenly getting all giggly. "He takes his time."

"Ohh, I like that. Well, introduce me to anyone I don't know." The two of them go off to the living room. I go back to the buffet table and start fussing with the food.

"Need any help, Lopi?" It's Tina.

"I'm almost done," I say, taking the tinfoil off a bowl of strawberries.

"You look great tonight," Tina says.

"Thanks," I mumble.

"Is anything wrong?"

"No." I flash a quick smile.

She refills my wineglass and raises hers in a toast. "To your mother," she says. "She knows how to throw a party." We clink our glasses and take a sip.

"You know all these people?" She waves her arm around. The place is filling up.

"Some," I say. "I think she invited her entire yoga class."

"Well, everyone loves Vivian. She's got more friends than anyone I know."

"Yeah," I say. "Is Josh here yet?" I ask as casually as I can.

"Haven't seen him. But he'll come. You can bet on it."

My mouth spreads in a great big grin just at the thought of him.

"Lopi," Tina lowers her voice. "I know how you feel about Josh."

"What?" I say, my smile struck down.

"It's written all over your face every time you see him," she says. "It's okay. I can understand why you have a crush on him. He is charming."

Crush, crush, crush. Why does everyone insist on using that word? A crush is not what I have at all. A crush is what I'd had on Peter Parkinson in the fourth grade when he threw wads of crumpled paper at me during Silent Sustained Reading. A crush is what someone gets on a movie star or someone they'll never know. I do not have a crush on Josh. We have something. He just doesn't know it yet, because he doesn't know how I feel. Tonight I will tell him and everything will change.

"You can talk to me anytime, Lopi," Tina says.

"All right," I say.

"I just want you to know that."

"All right," I say again. What, does she want me to start talking right now?

"I just don't want to see you get hurt is all."

"I won't," I say.

She raises her glass. "And go easy on the alcohol too. I will if you will. Deal?"

I nod and we toast once more.

Ten o'clock and Josh still hasn't arrived. My stomach is in knots, so I busy myself eating sesame gingersnaps and then start working on some of the more elaborate desserts. Somebody had the guts to bring a Cool Whip pie in a graham cracker crust. It must have been Viv's friend Barry— he would do something like that just for a joke. But it actually tastes pretty good. The whipped cream melts on my tongue and mixes with the crunching of the cracker crumbs. I pop a chocolate truffle to cleanse the pallet and then take another sip of wine. *I'll get high on sugar and wine,* I think. *Why not?*

I pretend I am a wine taster. I sniff it first then take a tiny sip and swish it around before deciding it meets my approval and taking a larger gulp. I am beginning to get upset that Josh still hasn't arrived. What if he doesn't come? I'll never get up the nerve again, or have an excuse to look this good.

I chat with some people, but I'm not fully there. My head nods in agreement, I mutter "fine" to their questions about school, and laughter even comes out, but all the time I am searching for Josh. Hoping for Josh.

Someone changes the music from a mellow background to a fast dance beat. Viv and Kenneth, an old BF who is now a good friend, move the furniture against the wall and start dancing. Soon a whole group is rocking in the living room. I sway a little to the beat and close my eyes.

Someone taps me on the shoulder and whispers in my ear, "May I have this dance?"

"Josh!" I say, turning around to face him. A few sandy curls drape over his eyes in such a way that makes me lose my balance. He steadies me by touching my elbow ever so slightly. "When did you get here?" I ask. *It's about time,* I think, *I've been waiting for you all night.*

"Just now. And I must say, if I'd known you were going to look so fine I would've arrived sooner."

I beam. How does he always know exactly what to say? Just then Tina comes by. "Hello, Josh."

"Tina, my darling, you look divine." He bows and kisses her hand.

"Yeah, whatever. Save it." She pushes up her cat-eye glasses that constantly slide down her nose.

"I mean it, Tina. You're all dressed up for Viv's party. Did you do laundry this month?"

"New jeans," she says, turning around to show off. Usually Tina wears T-shirts with stains and pants with big holes in them, often cut off and frayed at the bottom. She never gives much attention to what she wears and she never cares what anyone thinks, which makes everything look great on her.

"Lopi and I are going to cut the rug, but be sure to save one for me," he says.

"If you're lucky," Tina says, giving me a you-be-careful look.

I don't quite understand if Tina hates Josh or actually likes him. I know that Josh just flirts with her for fun. That's the way he is. But with me it is different. There is something meaningful in his eyes when he looks at me. He doesn't even look at Viv like that. We are meant to be together.

He pulls me into the living room and swings me around. Some people are dancing with themselves, some with partners. At school dances, which are bogus to begin with, all the girls dance in a group, but that is because so few guys my age dance anyway. Except for the obnoxious steady couples who dance slow and close so they can feel each other up. But Josh isn't some guy my age. He is mature.

Viv is still dancing with Kenneth and now Sandra, wiggling her butt and bending her knees down to the floor. She waves when she sees us and smiles. Josh blows her a kiss but doesn't go over. I'm sure that means he'd rather be with me.

He holds my hands tight and we stomp to the beat. This is it. I have to do it. I have to tell him and it has to be perfect. My head swirls with the motion and the music. He swings me close to him so that my mouth brushes against his ear.

Whisper it to him, now, I tell myself. Say it. But he has already swung me back out to arm's length. I smile. He grins, then lets go of my hand and turns around, gyrating his hips and flailing his arms about. It is a fast rockabilly tune. Too fast, I think. Not romantic enough. I'll wait for a better song.

But the next song isn't any better. I'll wait till we take a break. Then I'll tell him exactly how I feel. When Josh gets going he is a regular dancing machine. After five songs I finally yell, "I have to get a drink of water."

"What?" he shouts.

"I'm thirsty!" I mime drinking. He nods and keeps dancing.

I down two glasses at the kitchen sink. My ears are ringing and I am dizzy. I see an open bottle of liquor on the counter—I think it is rum—and pour some. *What the hell,* I think as I drink it fast, take a deep breath, and pour another. This night isn't working out like I had planned. I finish the rum and put the glass in the sink. I just have to tell him—then the rest will happen naturally. I straighten my shirt and charge back to the living room.

Tina is dancing with Barry and they call my name. I wave, but my arm feels like lead and it is a big effort.

I look for Josh and don't see him. Oh, no, he left. I panic, and then sigh with relief when I spot him by the front staircase, talking with Sandra. Viv is nowhere in sight. Perfect. I march toward him, falter a bit, and that's when I hear it. *Rrrrrip*. My pants. I look down and sure enough the seam in the crotch has come undone. Maybe if I walk with my legs together no one will notice. I am not about to let a little tear ruin my evening.

"Josh!" I call. It comes out louder than I expect. Sandra and Josh stop talking and stare at me. Can they tell? I lean against the railing and cross one leg over the other. I laugh, then take a breath. "Josh, I have to tell you something." There, so far so good. Now if I can just get him alone. Doesn't Sandra get the hint? I send her a mental note to take a hike.

"What, Lopi?" Josh asks.

"Up." I motion my head. "Stairs. Upstairs. Important." This isn't coming out right at all.

"Looks like she's ready for a good night's sleep and a whopper of a headache in the morning." Sandra's voice comes out of a fog.

What does she think, that I am drunk? Well, maybe the wine has gotten to me a little, but I still have all my wits about me. I take Josh's hand and stumble into him.

"I'd better get you to bed," he says. Yes, now he's talking.

I lead him upstairs. *See, I can walk just fine,* I think,

pissed at Sandra for making me look like a stupid fool. Then I remember my pants and try to walk with my legs together to conceal the rip.

"Do you have to go to the bathroom, Lopi?" Josh asks.

My face turns beet red—I know it does. "Noooo!" I laugh as if that is the funniest thing I've ever heard. "Just come here."

I get him into my room and close the door. I grab the clothes that are on the floor and shove them under the bed. I face him and cross my hands in front of my crotch, swaying from one foot to the other.

"Hey, hey, settle down. How much have you had to drink?"

"Not enough," I say. *Tell him, you fool,* I think. But the words won't come. Instead I begin unbuttoning my shirt. "Hot," I say, suddenly feeling it.

"Whoa. Hold on." He raises his hand. Before he can say anything else I grab him and kiss him hard on the mouth, or sort of near the mouth. I think it may be the side of his mouth and part of his cheek. I take his hand and put it inside my shirt. He keeps it there for a second; I know he does. Maybe even more than a second. Then he takes my hand and lifts it away from him.

"Listen, Lopi. You're drunk. Besides, I don't . . ."

I can't let him say the rest. "NO!" I shout. Say it, say it, oh why can't I just say it? Then he'll know and we'll tell Viv and she won't mind because she can always find another boyfriend and everything will be all right. But I can't get the damn words out. My stomach churns with desire and panic.

70

"I think you've had a long night. Maybe it's time for bed."

"But . . ." I begin. We hear people starting to sing "Happy Birthday" downstairs. They must have brought the cake out.

"I should be down there," Josh says. "It's Viv's big day."

"Wait!" If I don't do it now I never will. I take a great big breath. "Josh, I . . ." I take another breath and feel a sudden twinge in my stomach and a slight burning sensation in the back of my throat. I try to force the taste of wine and sesame gingersnaps and Cool Whip pie back into my stomach. I fling my arms around his neck and yell, "I love you!" just as the vomit reaches my mouth and I heave all over the back of Josh's beautiful striped shirt.

Gaslight

One, two, three days go by. I make it through school, but on Wednesday evening when Viv is in her pottery class, I punch in Josh's number then poise my finger over the Send button. Should I or shouldn't I? I hold my finger down ever so lightly, then harder. All of a sudden it goes through. I hang up just as fast. He'll be sure to see the number; it will come up missed on his cell phone. Why is this so hard? I've called guys before. I call Toad all the time. I've even called Josh before, but only if Viv has me relay some message, like "Lopi, call Josh and tell him to bring cream cheese to the brunch" or "Lopi, call Josh and ask him how to get this DVD to work."

Now Viv isn't around and I have no reason to call him except for my own. I punch in his number again and this time let it ring. If I am going to do this I'll have to get over my embarrassment.

"Hello?" His voice catches me off-guard.

"Uh . . . hi . . . " I stutter.

"Lopi?"

"It's me," I say.

"Oh, hey, Lopi, I almost didn't recognize you. What's up?"

Suddenly the whole party comes back to me. The wine, the desire, the stupidity. My stupidity. Maybe I should just pretend it never happened, or better yet, that I can't remember anything. I can always feign innocence.

"You there, Lopi?" Maybe he won't even mention the party.

"Yeah."

"Are you feeling okay?"

"Yeah, why?"

"Well, you were a little out of it the last time I saw you."

"I was?" Innocence.

"You were. You must have woken with a doozie. Don't you remember coming on to me?"

Oh, god. "Uh . . . I don't remember much."

"Well, you had a lot of wine, my dear. And it went straight to your pretty little head. You honestly don't remember?"

"I remember dancing and eating a lot of chocolate."

"Yeah, well, that came out on my shirt. But never mind. Everyone's got to experience their first time. Might as well be at your mother's birthday party."

"Did I do anything stupid?" Keep feigning.

"Nothing out of the ordinary. Forget it. So what's on your mind?"

"Well, I was wondering—I mean, if you'd like to . . . Well, there's this movie playing. You might like it. And, well, maybe you'd like to see it." I stop. He doesn't say anything, so I go on, "With me. I want to see it and I thought you'd like it, since you're always talking about old movies. And it's in town now. Tonight's the last night, but, well, if you can't go I'm going to go anyway. I want to see it."

"Lopi?" Josh says.

"Yeah?"

"What's the movie?"

"Oh, right. That might help. It's called *Gaslight*. With Ingrid Bergman. It's really old. Black and white. It's at the Star Theatre. It's supposed to be good."

"Sure, sounds like fun."

"Really? I mean, yeah, great, it does sound like fun." I am such an idiot.

"What about Viv? Does she want to come?"

I frown. No. Viv most definitely does NOT want to come. If Josh doesn't remember that she has a class tonight, I'm not going to remind him. "I'll ask. Maybe."

"Is there a seven o'clock showing? I'll pick you guys up at quarter of, okay?"

"We actually have some errands downtown. Let's meet there." Quick thinking on my part.

"Okay. See you then."

"See you."

And we have a date.

I sit on the bench in the lobby of the Star Theatre. It is six-thirty. I should have brought a book to read so it doesn't look like I am obviously waiting and obviously early. I had to leave the house fast, before Viv got back, so I wouldn't have to explain anything to her. Or lie. Now I'll just have to white lie to Josh. I busy myself reading the movie schedule for the fifth time.

"Hey, Lopi!" I jump happily, expecting Josh, but it is Toad, red-faced and grinning. "You're seeing *Gaslight*. Cool."

"Yeah, I suppose."

"We can sit together."

I love how he just assumes I am alone. Like I can't possibly be on a date.

"Well, I'm sort of already sitting with someone."

Toad looks around. How dare he not believe me. And why is he seeing this movie anyway? No one in school goes to the Star.

"Who?" he asks.

"A friend."

"You have friends?"

I am insulted. "Yes," I say.

"You haven't had friends for years. Is it Karen?"

"No," I say.

"That girl Apple you've been hanging out with?"

"No, forget it. You don't know him."

"Him? Like a date? Are you on a date, Lopi? Where is he? I'll check him out for you."

"It's not a date," I say. "It's just a movie with a guy I know." The last thing I want is for Toad to see Josh. I'd made the mistake of telling Toad a little too much about getting drunk at Viv's party, how cute I think Josh is, and that I wanted to have sex with him.

Toad finally guesses. "It's not Josh, is it?"

I don't answer, which is an answer in itself.

"Oh, Lopi. Not him. Not that guy." Toad shakes his head. "What are you going to do—try to seduce him again? Here in the movie theater? That's disgusting. Besides, he is your mother's boyfriend."

"Shhh. Keep your voice down. I'm not seducing him. I told you, I was drunk that night."

"Oh, right, and I've been meaning to talk to you about that. Drinking is a nasty habit. Nasty habits don't suit you, Lopi."

"You don't know anything about anything!"

"Whatever." Toad shrugs. "It's your life. I just care a little bit, that's all. You're my friend."

"Well, I didn't sign up to be your friend."

"You're changing, Lopi, and not for the better."

"Nobody asked you to care." This is mean. I know it. Toad doesn't deserve it, but he is always so affected by everything. So sensitive. Like a baby I have to tiptoe around. I am tired of tiptoeing and trying to protect Toad's feelings all the time.

"Where is the guy? Maybe he's standing you up?"

"He'll be here," I say. *He'd better be here,* I think. Though how am I going to get Toad to leave? Toad is like mold. He attaches himself to you and then spreads.

"Aren't you going to get your ticket?" I ask.

"Someone's got to stay and make sure you're going to be okay. I want to check this guy out. Make sure he's good enough for you."

"Don't do me any favors."

"It's not for you. I'm curious who you're going to lose your virginity to, that's all."

"Shhh, not so loud."

"Where are you planning on doing it, by the way? At your house? Won't that be weird if your mother walks in? His car? God, I couldn't imagine having sex in a car—how uncomfortable. Is that your penis or the stick shift poking me?" Toad laughs at his own joke. I can't believe that he actually said the word *penis*. Toad, who is terrified of anything related to sex. I bury my head in the movie schedule and pretend I don't know him. He goes on, ignoring me ignoring him. "I'd make him take you to his place. Although that could be unsafe. What if he turns out to be a rapist or a murderer?"

I roll my eyes. "It can't be rape if it's mutual," I say.

"It can too. He could make you do things you don't want to do. Don't do anything you don't want to do, Lopi. I'm concerned for your safety. You're not thinking clearly."

"You're just jealous," I say.

"Am not. You can do it with whoever you want."

"I am not an idiot, Toad."

"I know, but it's crazy out there."

"He's not some stranger."

"You don't know what happens to people when they get sexed up. It brings out all sorts of inner secrets."

"How would you know?" I ask. Yet it is those very secrets that I want to uncover. I want to see the inside of people. I want someone to see the inside of me.

Just then I spot Josh, running down the hall, his curls bobbing. My heart flips.

"This conversation is over and never to be repeated," I whisper to Toad, giving him the eye. "Not to a soul, or you are dead meat."

"Okay, okay." Toad raises his arms in defense. "I just have one word for you." He leans in and whispers, "Condoms," then stands back, looking as though he just gave me the answer to world peace.

"Lopi! Hope you haven't been waiting long!" Josh pecks me on the cheek, and I glow inside.

"I just got here." I glance at Toad, who stands next to me like a lump. A lump of mold. Great, now I have to introduce them. "Josh, this is Toad. He goes to my school."

For a second I have this fantasy of them both being my lovers and not knowing it. I shake my head and concentrate on Josh's lower lip. I want to trace my finger over that lip and nibble on it. Toad and Josh shake hands and say the usual cordial things to each other.

"Where's Viv?" Josh asks, looking around.

"She couldn't come," I say, hoping Toad won't chime in. He raises his eyebrows at me and lets out a slight guffaw, which he turns into a cough. I want to smack him.

"Oh." Josh's eyelids droop and flutter with disappointment. "We'd better get our tickets, then."

We all stand there awkwardly. I silently plead with Toad to leave. And, bless him, the mold gets the message.

"I changed my mind," he says. "I've seen this movie

already, and I just remembered I have to start an English paper. You've probably done all your homework already, Lopi." Toad turns to Josh. "Lopi's graduating this year. She's too smart for the rest of us lowlifes."

I could just die, but I give a grateful thank-you nod to Toad for leaving.

"You're a riot," Josh says, laughing. "I'm sure I'll see you again. Tad, was it?"

"Toad," Toad corrects. He saunters down the hall with his hands in his pockets. I actually feel a little sorry for him. It's hard to be the third wheel. I certainly know first-hand what that's like. At least he has the decency to leave. I give him credit for knowing where he's not wanted.

"He seems like a great kid. A real crackup," Josh says as Toad disappears around the corner.

"I've known him forever. He's okay. Kind of immature." I don't want Josh to get the wrong idea about Toad and me. I touch his elbow. "Come on. Let's go in."

I try to concentrate on the movie, but I am too aware of Josh beside me. I keep thinking about our almost kiss at the party. Then thoughts of Toad creep into my head, and every once in a while Viv gets in there too. Maybe losing my virginity with Josh isn't the way to go. But I want to at least try. I have to try. I know we have something special. The way he looks at me and uses any excuse to touch me, even just a subtle touch.

Like in the movie theater, a couple of times his shoulder rubs against mine, and neither one of us pulls away. I can feel his energy through the fabric of his shirt and it is electrifying. It is all I can do to restrain myself from grabbing his arm and pulling him close. I want his body on top of mine, his lips pressing into me. I imagine his breath quickening as he nibbles my ear and murmurs "I love you."

I keep my hand readily available in case he wants to hold it. When he leans forward in his seat I stare at his back. I think about rubbing it, massaging his neck, running my fingers through his hair. I imagine him with no shirt. I've seen him shirtless before. He has a great back. Well developed, but not overly muscular. A good, straight back. A little hair on his chest to twirl, but not hairy by any means. I sigh. How can I go through with this? How can I not go through with it?

He leans back and whispers in my ear. "What a horrific life." At first I think he means my life, but then I realize it has to do with the movie. I nod in the dark.

I am relieved when the movie is finally over. It is too painful to think about touching him but not daring. I need to know what he thinks. Yet I don't want to ruin it by making a move he isn't ready for, like the last time.

Josh gives me a ride home. He talks about *Gaslight* the whole way. "Finally I know what it means to gaslight someone. What a great movie! They don't make movies that psychologically interesting anymore. Nothing with character. It's all blow 'em up and smash 'em down, or else Hollywood romantic sap. God, if I never see another chick flick again in my life I'll die happy."

I pretend that I absorbed the film as intensely as I'd absorbed his back, arm, neck. Before I know it we pull in the driveway behind the Volvo. "Yay!" Josh says, his face lighting up for the first time all night. "Viv is home."

Is this all? Am I going to let the evening fall through the cracks yet again? Drunk or not drunk, it doesn't make a difference. I still can't say what I want to say.

"About the party . . ." I start.

"Oh, that. Don't worry about it. You had too much to drink. We all have to go through that. Besides, I had the shirt dry-cleaned. It's fine."

"About what I said . . ." I pause while he fiddles with the car keys. "I meant it. I want to sleep with you. I love you."

As soon as the words are out of my mouth I know it is all wrong. Josh doesn't look happy; he doesn't even look surprised. His face falls, as though this is the worst news he could receive.

He finally says my name. "Lopi." Suddenly I am ashamed. I feel dirty. He shakes his head and his eyes turn red and begin to brim at the corners. His body heaves in small waves. "Lopi, don't . . ."

I don't expect this. Telling me I am too young, or not pretty enough, that it will never work, maybe. I want him to at least kiss me or touch me. Instead he turns teary. We sit there, miles apart.

"I love Vivian," he finally says. "I'm going to ask her to marry me."

This is not part of my fantasy at all.

Imagining a Kiss

I have a fantasy kiss scene. I don't know where exactly it takes place, maybe in a college dorm room, and I don't know who the guy is, but I can see it clear as day and I can feel it as though it is actually happening. It goes something like this:

I am waiting outside a door, his door. My heart is thumping in my throat. My pulse is racing with the thrill of just being there, in the hallway close to him. I feel brazen. I knock.

He opens the door and smiles. I grin at the sight of him. His long legs in shorts. Everything about him is so right. My body screams. He pulls me in and we kiss. Long, wet, breathless, passionate.

We take a breath and I say, "I can't believe I'm here. I can't believe you're you." He puts a finger to my lips and kisses me again. My neck, my shoulders, my eyelids.

"Lie down," he says, motioning to the bed.

I lie on top of him and we keep kissing. I could kiss him forever. "Kissing is nice," I say in between kisses.

"It's great," he says.

"Not enough kissing in the world," I whisper.

He nods and we kiss some more.

I'm sure that Elwood the Shrink would explain what all this meant. Why I can imagine stuff so clearly, but why I can't seem to do any of it in reality.

Lies

Apple is at my house, in my room, looking at my things. We met in the park, and this time I was able to run most of the way with her. It was too cold to stand around outside chatting in our running clothes after, so she basically invited herself over.

"Your room is so neat and tidy." She wanders around checking out my things. She studies the goldfish on the bookshelf. Ever since I can remember I've had a pet fish. When one dies I get a new one and always name him the same thing. This one is George the twelfth. Apple taps George's bowl, then hops onto my desk, swinging her legs over the edge. I am on the bed. Tessa jumps up and noses me to pet her.

I spend a lot of time in my room, and in contrast to the rest of the house I have very little clutter. Besides, I just cleaned it last night. Whenever I can't sleep I clean my room or organize my desk. I like having my things just so.

"It must be great to be an only child. No one getting in

your way," Apple says. She has three younger sisters. "And your mom is so cool. She lets you do anything."

I nod. Everyone thinks this. On the outside my mother is cool and she does trust me to do whatever I want. I am for the most part trustworthy, on the outside, anyway. On the outside everything looks great.

Apple glances at the paper on my desk. "Is this your English paper on that monumental novel we just finished? Man, that took forever." Apple reads the title, "'Evil Wins the Race: Why I Disagree with John Steinbeck.' Heavy," she says. "Mrs. V.O. loves it when people disagree, as long as you can back it up."

"Hmm." I don't really feel like talking about this with Apple. I don't think she'd fully understand. Thankfully, she puts the paper down. English is not Apple's favorite class. She's in the AP class, but she just barely skims by. I think she reads the online Cliff Notes instead of the book. I am a little embarrassed about my paper on *East of Eden*. It's really depressing, about how evil takes over and destroys everything. It kind of goes against what Steinbeck says, but when I wrote it I found myself believing it. I can't wait to see how Mrs. V.O. reacts.

Apple's eye catches the painting over the bookshelf. It is hard to miss. I painted it last year when I was miserable in school—actually, it was after this painting that I decided I had to get out early. Apple goes over to examine it more closely.

"This is a creepy painting. Did you do it? It looks like you, in a creepy way."

It is an image of a girl's face, not a self-portrait exactly, but there is maybe some similarity. This girl's hair is much darker than mine and sticking up in all directions. Her eyes are almost hollow, with yellow centers, and her mouth is exaggerated so that it spills off her face. I didn't intend for her to be me. Her face is peering from behind bars—heavy, dark bars—with two howling dogs at the bottom. Above the barred window is a bird flying into the distance. The dogs' teeth, the girl's eyes, the bird, and the full moon are the only hints of light in the whole piece.

"I didn't know you were into art," Apple says.

"I'm not, really. I took an art elective last year," I say.

Apple's face registers a memory and she exclaims, "Hey, I was in that elective for like a nanosecond. It looked like it was going to be a lame class—making animal sculpture out of bars of soap."

"It was kind of sad. We had to draw baskets of peaches and pineapples too."

Apple grunts. "This school needs more art, less sport. Less competitive sport, anyway. I have nothing against athletics." She looks back at the painting. "You should go to art school. Seriously—you're good. There's a lot of feeling in here."

"Thanks," I say. This is the nicest thing anyone has ever said about my painting. Viv shakes her head in dismay every time she sees it, which is rarely, since she never comes into my room. Her paintings from her watercolor class are all pretty flowers and ocean scenes with bobbing boats on the horizon.

Apple goes back to my desk and this time sits in the swivel chair. She picks out a pencil from the mug and plays with it between her fingers. "So who do you think is hot in the senior class?"

I pause a minute. "No one, really. I like older guys. Though that guy Charley in English is okay."

"Charley is hot, kind of adorable, actually, but he's almost too perfect—they're the most boring. I know what you mean about older guys. Living so close to Concord, you must see gorgeous college boys all the time."

"Why do you think I study at the library there?"

"We'll have to go to the frat parties at the beginning of the semester. Or whatever they are now." The frats at Concord were all obliterated a few years ago after two freshmen died during rush week. One was found naked in the bushes, suffocated in his own vomit. The other jumped off the roof and snapped her neck—no one knew if she had been told to jump or if she did it on her own. It was a huge ordeal, and so they shut down all frats and the rituals and rules associated with them. Now they are just communal houses for students. Practically the same thing.

"Don't you have a college student living here?" Apple asks. "Can't she hook you up with someone?"

"Tina's older. She keeps pretty separate from the school."

"Too bad. But seriously, would you do it with Charley?"

I think about that. Charley is one of those perfect people. I don't know if he'd even be interested in someone evil like me. I do notice that he watches me sometimes in class.

Maybe he thinks I am a freak, but he's got a great smile, and it doesn't look like an I-think-you-are-a-freak smile. "I might," I say.

"Who have you done it with? How many?"

My insides tighten. I knew that eventually Apple would ask this. What am I going to say? How can I admit that I've never actually had sex? Like all good embarrassed, insecure teenagers, I lie and say, "I've slept with two guys." Two seems reasonable. And it could be true. "One was in high school and one wasn't."

"Oh, do tell!" Apple puts the pencil down and leans forward.

"The older guy was a few months ago, but he's not in town anymore."

"Transferred?"

"Yeah. He was a freshman at the college and hated it. Left after the first month. I think he went to California. It was only a fling." The more I lie, the easier it gets.

"Was he good?"

I give her a blank look.

"The sex. How was it?"

"Oh, good, he was good."

Apple looks disappointed so I give her more. "We met while I was walking Tessa last August. He was moving into his dorm and Tessa grabbed his bagel. We did it mainly in his dorm room when his roommate was gone. He knew what to do."

Apple seems pleased with this. "What about the high school guy? Is it your friend, the one with the funny name you always hang out with? What is his name?" I let her try to remember and she does. "Toad! That's it! I knew I knew it. So is it him?"

I don't want to verbalize this lie, but I make my face let her believe she guessed right. Toad and I have shared a bed several times, when we were younger and I used to stay with him when Viv went away for her long weekends. So we have slept together, but literally, not figuratively. Once our legs touched by mistake.

"Really? I thought he'd be gay."

"He's not," I say.

"He is pretty hot, for a junior. He's got that sexy long hair like the elfin in *Lord of the Rings*. Was he good? Did he even know what to do? He seems a little clumsy."

"He was good," I say. I don't want to give Toad a bad reputation. It's bad enough that I am giving him a reputation at all, but maybe it will be good for him.

"Do you still do it with him?"

"No, we're just friends, now. It's better that way. He's kind of like my brother. I stayed with him for a while when my mom was away. It was just too weird to keep doing it."

"I know what you mean. He was your first, right? You never forget your first. Mine was a jerk, but I'll never forget him."

"Yeah, I guess I've been lucky. Both of mine were fine."

"Do you mind if I make a try for Toad? Is he fair game?"

Now what could I say? I'd dug myself in this deep. Would Toad even go for Apple? Would she be the one to seduce him and not me? I didn't even want to do it with Toad, but now maybe I should rethink that.

"No, that's okay," I say. "Go for it."

That Special Place

Somewhere around twelve years old I began thinking about sex. I started touching myself and masturbating. I'm not sure exactly how I figured it out—it's not like anyone told me how to do it or why to do it. I'd read some book where the girl touches herself in a "special place" and it made her feel good, though it never said where that special place was. For a while I thought maybe it was under her arm, or behind her knee, or possibly her breasts. The thought that it was between her legs somehow seemed impossible. I still don't know why the author never came right out and said it—did she think everyone would automatically know? Maybe I was too young when I read the book, but it did make me wonder.

When I lie in bed I start to think about something really sexy—scenes from movies sometimes, but usually something I've made up—some story where a guy seduces a girl and they go at it. I imagine someone touching me—I try to feel their breath on me, their hands exploring my body. I pretend my hands are his hands. I reach under the covers and touch my "special place," which by the way is called a vagina—one of those taboo words. People say *penis* all the time, but never *vagina,* and especially not *clitoris,* as if they are forbidden, evil words. *Vagina, clitoris, vagina.*

The only thing I can never figure out is why, while it does feel good, afterward I always cry—sometimes for a long time. I can't help it. It makes me sad in a weird way. Even sadder than usual. However, I still do it. It's like I want to feel that sadness. I am such a weirdo. I don't know if I'll ever be normal. I mean, what would some guy do if I get all blubbery on him right after having his penis in me? It's not exactly giving someone a good impression.

English Existentialism

Mrs. V.O. keeps me after class. She has my paper on *East of Eden* in her hand. "You haven't been yourself lately, Penelope."

I stare at my shoes.

She looks at me askew, and goes on: "And this paper isn't like what you usually write."

"I thought it was good." I did. I thought what I wrote was full of insight and profound ideas. I had written it on Steinbeck's theme of good and evil. Near the end of the book he states that people have a never-ending contest in themselves between good and evil, and that the good will live on after we die, but that the evil needs to constantly regenerate. Basically I disagreed with him. Even though the "evil" character in the book kills herself, her evil actions still go on.

"It's well written, sure. But I'm not so sure that you believe what you wrote. Do you really think that there is no chance for good in this world?"

"Sometimes," I say. "Look at all the bad things . . . all the wars, bombs, people who kill people."

"Yes, that's one way to see things, but there is good too? Can you see that? I think what Steinbeck is saying is that both exist and that we can learn to emphasize one over the other."

"You're the one who always says don't believe everything just because it's written down."

"It's fine to disagree with Steinbeck. I'm just not sure you really do."

I don't say anything. I watch a bird perch on the maple tree outside.

"Is everything okay with you, Penelope?"

"Sure," I say.

"How is your mother?" Mrs. V.O. knows Viv from a poetry class Viv took with her one summer through continuing ed. Viv also knows Mr. Van Orton, who had a kidney transplant a few years ago. Viv was his nurse. There are few secrets in our town.

"She's fine," I say.

Mrs. V.O. studies me a while longer. "And you are running for Mr. Koch? How's that going?"

"Good. I actually like running. I'm getting better. I run with Apple sometimes."

"Glad to hear it. How about colleges? Have you applied?"

"I have the applications. I'm applying to two. I want to go to the smaller alternative one."

"I think you have a lot of potential, Lopi. You're smart

enough to graduate early, but you can do more than that. You can go far, but you need to think about what you say—say what you mean. How's the personal essay for your application coming?"

"I haven't exactly started it," I admit sheepishly. "But I think I want to write it on existentialism in the modern world, in my world."

We started studying existentialism recently and something about it really clicked with me. The French existentialists have some really interesting ideas about the arbitrariness of life. It's this idea that a bunch of writers, philosophers, and artists came up with in the 1940s that life really is meaningless. That what we do in the end doesn't matter, that from the moment we are born we have a death sentence and there is nothing we can do about it other than live our lives. This sounds like it could be really depressing, but when you think about it, it's actually uplifting. Sometimes I think we place way too much emphasis on the meaning of life and leaving our mark. What if there really is no plan laid out for us, no fate, no future? What if things just happen and then we die? We might as well make the most of it, then. I find this idea far more freeing than the idea that we supposedly have to do something really important, as if what we are doing already isn't important. I tell Mrs. V.O. a little about this and get more excited as I explain it to her.

"That's good, Lopi. I can see you have ideas, you are a good thinker. Keep thinking, and you'll sort out the other. Let me know if you need help, with the paper or with anything else."

"Thanks," I say.

"You know, talking to Ms. Stein might help too."

I doubt it, I think, but I nod okay to Mrs. V.O.

"And give my best to your mom." She hands me my paper.

When I get to my locker I read the grade. I got an A–. There is a personal note from Mrs. V.O. in her scratchy handwriting: *Nice work, but do you really think this? I wish you could believe that things are not all that bad. Chin up.*

I guess I'll have to keep my papers safe for Mrs. V.O. from now on.

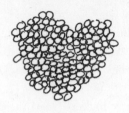

Party with the Rabbits

Time passes and I keep waiting for Viv to tell me about Josh's proposal, but she doesn't. Did she say yes? No? Did Josh even ask her yet? I don't dare bring it up. I avoid Josh when he comes over. I can't bare the thought of looking him in the eye and thinking he could be my stepfather. I avoid Toad too because I know he'll give me an I told-you-so. So when Apple invites me to crash a Concord party, I instantly say yes.

Apple is a pro at crashing college parties. "It's all in the attitude. Just walk right in like no one cares. Act like you belong."

I wear black jeans with a low-cut black sweater, and dab a glitter brush over my neck and cheeks. I puff up my hair and stick out my chest in my college student look. This will be good practice, since with any luck I will be one soon.

The party is in one of the former frat houses, a ten-minute walk away. Now the buildings are considered communal housing, and none of the jocks lives there anymore.

There are still wild parties thrown, but without any authoritative approval, which makes them wilder in some ways.

There are a few people dotted around the porch, wearing puffy down jackets and smoking cigarettes. They nod at us as we pass. Apple has dyed her hair a dark shade of blue. It shines iridescent in the dim lights of the living room. It's not very crowded and the living room is spacious, with high ceilings and comfortable old couches pushed against the walls. There is a long table by the fireplace with a bowl of something that looks like lemonade, and a keg on the floor. There are bowls of chips and popcorn strewn about. A mini stereo on the mantel booms out reggae. All in all, it is tamer than Viv's parties. No dancing, just a lot of standing and sitting around.

A few people nod to us as Apple leads me to the keg. Before we get a drink, the sweet smell of pot wafts to our nostrils.

"Mmm. Let's find that," Apple says, with her nose in the air like a dog catching a scent. We follow the smell into a smaller room off the living room—a sitting room, maybe, in the old days. I do a quick survey. There is a group of ten or so seated on various chairs, couch, floor. About half notice us; the rest are engrossed in conversation. More boys than girls—seven to three.

I lock eyes with a cute boy in the corner on the floor. A girl is talking to him, but he is looking at me. He has a round, boyish face. He looks young to be in college, but then some guys keep that boyish look their entire lives. His body isn't round; rather, he looks tall and bony the way he is sitting with his back curved and his crossed knees jutting out awkwardly. To compensate for his boyish face he is trying to grow some sort of goatee. He has sweet almond eyes. I flash a smile then look away.

"Well, hello there," a guy from the couch says. He is all eyes for Apple. "Make room for new blood." He squeezes the three guys next to him to the end of the couch, forcing one to get up, and pats the newly formed empty space next to him. Apple plops herself down. I sit on the armrest.

"You're new, huh? Freshmen?" the guy asks. He is definitely the most attractive in the room. With dark hair and eyes, he looks Latin.

Apple laughs. "No, actually we're seniors."

"Get out of town! I've never seen you before, either of you. And I get around."

"We don't go to this school." Apple laughs again. She loves this. Apple is the one person who can make a flirtatious game out of the truth.

"Ah." The guy seems satisfied with this answer. He fills in the blanks. "Visiting friends, then?"

"You could say that. If you're willing to be my friend, then we are visiting you." Apple bats her eyes.

"That might be possible," the guy says. "I'm Chip." He hands her the joint he's been holding.

"Apple," Apple says.

They both look at me, waiting.

"Lopi," I say. "Short for Penelope."

Apple inhales the joint, holds it, and then releases with a little puff. She hands it to me.

This is my first time. Apple doesn't know this. Even Viv

probably assumes I've been smoking pot for years. She wouldn't object to my smoking, just as long as I didn't take hers. "Pot is better than alcohol," she says. "There's no reason it should be illegal." She even has LEGALIZE MARIJUANA stickers that she sticks on the back of her bill envelopes (when she pays them). I can just imagine what the electric company must think when they see that.

I bring the joint to my mouth. I know to hold it in— don't be a wimp and exhale right away. My lungs fill with burning smoke. My head begins to blur from holding. I need to cough, but I don't want people to know I haven't done this before. I can't hold it anymore and finally erupt in a coughing explosion. Everyone stares at me.

"You okay there?" Chip says.

I nod.

Apple pats my back like it's no big deal. "It's strong stuff," she says. I muffle out a yup, and, still coughing, hand the joint to the girl next to me. The conversation drifts back to normal and I stifle any more coughs, though they keep slipping out in mini aftershocks.

Apple leans over to Chip and I hear her whisper, "Don't worry about her."

Chip opens his stoned eyes wide. "I'm not worried." He examines Apple carefully. "Hey, you've got blue hair!"

Apple shakes her head in his face. "I do?"

"Is it real?"

"Touch it and see."

He reaches over and rubs her head. "Hey, cool. So soft. You must use conditioner. Are you an art major?"

"Could be."

The two of them go off into a conversation, if you can call it that, about art school education versus liberal arts. Chip is apparently a psychology major—go figure.

Everyone has broken off into their own circles, in pairs or threesomes. I am the only one left out, besides round-faced, cute boy on the floor, who is not paying attention to the girl talking to him but instead is staring at me.

I don't look at him except for an occasional glimpse out of my peripheral. I mentally send him messages to come talk to me. Finally he gets them. He walks over and stands next to me. "Hi," he says.

I open my mouth to say hi back but start up again with a coughing fit.

"Hold on," he says. He goes into the other room and comes back with a glass of water.

"Here."

I take the water. It's cold and slippery. The most delicious water I have ever had. I never thought water could taste so good. I empty the glass in one long gulp and hand it back to him. "Thanks."

"Do you need more?" he asks.

I don't want him to think I am ordering him around, but I do want more. I nod. He leaves again and this time he is gone for longer. I think he may not return; he probably thinks I am some first-time-smoking-pot loser. I listen to Apple tell Chip about her hair color choice. She leans in to him and he puts his arm around her. How does she move so fast? After eons, my round-faced boy returns, this time balancing two glasses and a bowl of pretzels.

He sits in front of me and watches as I down the second

glass. He hands me the other one, but I shake my head. "I'm okay. That was great water."

We look at each other and don't say anything. His eyes curve up when he smiles.

"What are you studying?" he asks.

Apple is thoroughly engaged in her conversation with Chip and the other guy and girl on the couch, not paying any attention to me, so I lie. "Philosophy." It might be true. It might be what I major in. I certainly ponder the meaning of life enough to qualify.

He nods as though this makes sense.

"You look like a philosopher. As if there's a lot going on in there." He taps my head three times with his finger.

The joint makes its way back to me and I hold it, wondering if I should give it another try. I don't feel stoned yet.

Round-faced boy hands me the other glass of water. "Try taking a sip first."

I do. The smoke is easier to hold with my throat coated with cool water. I only cough slightly this time.

The boy tells me his name is Andrew. He is a freshman and wants to major in English. Maybe be a writer.

"You must be a sophomore if you've picked a major already," he says.

"What do you want to write?" I ask.

"I'm not sure. Personal memoir stuff, maybe."

"Don't you have to have a memorable life for that?"

"Maybe I do."

I laugh at this, but I don't pry. I suppose we all have memorable lives in our way. He looks as if he may have suffered some already—or maybe it's just that he's quiet and I am drawn to him. I don't think I can be drawn to normal, happy, well-adjusted people. Like Chip, for example. He seems so perfect, and yet I'm not interested in him. Though it looks like Apple is.

"Do you want to go outside?" Andrew asks. "It's a beautiful night."

"Sure."

I tell Apple I am going. "Just tell me if you're going to leave." She winks at me. I pretend I don't notice.

Andrew and I sit on the porch steps. The night is black with a few hazy clouds circling the almost full moon. We are in the midst of a winter thaw, and there is the fresh smell of melting snow. It is brisk but clean. I wrap my arms around myself.

"So what is your philosophy of life, Penelope?"

"Lopi. Everyone calls me Lopi. No one ever calls me Penelope, except Mrs. V.O."

"Who?" he asks.

I stop myself. I can't say that Mrs. V.O. is my English teacher. My high school English teacher. I already indicated that I go to school here. He thinks I am a sophomore. "Someone from home," I quickly explain.

He waits. He is waiting for my philosophy. Suddenly it strikes me that this is a very funny question. Suddenly it strikes me that I am out of it. Not totally, but just enough to feel pretty good.

"What is my philosophy of life?" I repeat and break out in the giggles. He laughs with me, then stops and looks at me. As though he is staring into my brain. I rumple his hair. "Who are you?" I ask.

"I'm Andrew," he says. "That's who."

"Okay," I say. "That's good enough for me."

"Now tell me."

"Tell you what?" I suppress more laughter. I feel good. I feel happy. The night is beautiful. I am flirting with a cute boy.

"You know."

"Oh, right. Philosophy. After all, that's my major, so I should have one. A philosophy, that is. As well as a life. I mean, we all have a life, until we don't. Then we have death. And who's to say that's worse: Life can be pretty bad sometimes. I mean, sometimes it's so lonely, it is suffocating. You know what I mean? But like now, now is a beautiful time to be alive. This very second. It's so beautiful. The sky, the moon, the clouds. The air. Doesn't it smell good? How can things ever be bad when it smells this good?" I pause, breathe. "I think I am stoned," I say.

"I think so," he says, laughing. "It's nice, isn't it?" He puts his arm around me and I snuggle in. We sit like that. I fit under his arm like a hand in a mitten. Everything is perfect. He is my perfect round-faced boy. I think I am in love.

"I have rabbits," he blurts suddenly.

We both laugh hysterically.

"What?" I finally say when I catch my breath.

"I have rabbits in my room. Two of them."

I start to laugh again. "That's what I thought you said."

"Do you want to see them?" he asks.

"Oh, this is just a ploy to get me to come to your room. I'm onto you." I wag my finger, touch his shoulder.

"No, really — I mean it."

"Prove it."

"I live on the other side of campus. In Smith House."

"I know Smith House — it's right near . . ." I stop myself before I say my house. I stand up a little too fast and teeter off-balance. I put out my hand. "Okay, Mr. Andrew. Take me to your rabbits."

He takes my hand and we walk down the stairs with our fingers intertwined, every finger releasing energy between us. I can feel his pulse and my pulse through our fingers combining to make one pulse. I just met this guy and I like him. Forget Josh, forget Viv, forget Toad. It is that easy.

As we reach the street I suddenly remember Apple. I can't leave without telling her. "Stay right here. Don't move an inch." I unlock our fingers and run back inside. It takes me a minute to find her. I finally spot her blue head in the kitchen, bobbing above the open refrigerator door. Chip and some others are with her.

"There you are, girl," she says when she sees me. She puts her arm around my shoulder. "Having fun?"

"I'm going to go see that guy's rabbits."

This sends Apple into a tizzy of laughter. "Oh, rabbits, eh?"

One of the girls she is with eyes us suspiciously. "Is that Andrew you're talking about?" she asks.

I look at her. She has dark hair in pigtails.

"He has rabbits," I say.

"Yeah, right. That's what he thinks." The girl narrows her eyes. I have instant disdain for her.

"Hey, don't you have rabbits too, Louise?" someone asks.

"Yeah, I've got rabbits."

Apple and I look at each other. We shrug our shoulders and laugh at the absurdity of things.

"Oh, well," I say.

"Have fun," Apple says.

"Have fun," the pigtailed girl named Louise echoes, and shakes her head, as if I am the butt of some joke.

I make my way back through the living room, ducking in and out of circles of people. I finally get to the porch and don't see Andrew anywhere.

He's gone! He left me!

"Looking for your boyfriend?" someone on the porch rail says. I nod. I don't bother denying the boyfriend comment. Let them think what they want. Thinking is not a crime. I follow the guy's finger.

Andrew is lying in the melted snow near a row of hedges with his arms stretched out. I stand over him.

"Hey, you," he says. He reaches over my boots and up my pant legs and begins to rub my calves. "Such nice legs." His breath condenses in the cold.

"What about the rabbits?" I say.

"Right." He gets up.

We walk across campus, holding hands. He tells me about his life and why he wants to write a memoir. Turns out he does have an interesting life. His parents were gypsies and they lived with his ten brothers and sisters in an

RV that they drove all over the country, getting kicked out of town after town for not having a housing permit. Half his siblings were on crack, and the other half went to prison or got pregnant. When he was old enough he left and worked on his own. He managed to finish high school and apply to Concord. I listen in amazement. Some people really do have interesting lives. Mine seems normal in comparison—provincial, at any rate. Crazy mother. Absent father. Dead brother.

"So, that's enough about me," he says. "And you?"

I don't think I can carry on my lie, but I don't want to tell him the truth and have him be mad or, worse, think I am insincere. "Let's save me for another time," I say.

We keep walking and silence takes over. We are going back to his room. We may have sex. Am I prepared for this? Is he the one? I begin to hear everyone's voices in my head.

Toad: "I have one word: condoms."

Josh: "I knew you had a crush on someone!"

Viv: "It's about time my daughter got laid, and stoned. All in one night!"

Tina: "Sex is just another way to have fun, like dancing."

Mrs. V.O.: "Remember, a blowjob is sex. Oral sex is still sex, no matter what people say."

Even my imaginary Elwood the Shrink gets a word in: "Is this really what you want?"

All their voices are in my head at once. "Shut up," I say.

"What?" Andrew asks. I must have said it out loud.

"Nothing. I didn't mean you."

We stop in front of a white clapboard house. A sign above the door reads SMITH HOUSE, CONCORD COLLEGE.

"Here we are," he says.

He leads me through the door, down a hall, and up a flight of stairs. We walk to the end of the hall and he unlocks a door.

"Come on in." He guides me inside with his hand centered on my back.

He is right about the rabbits. There is a large cage on top of the dresser, and inside, two fat rabbits are wriggling their noses.

I run over to them. "Cute," I say. "Well, sort of." One of them is very large, the size of an obese cat. He or she is dirty white, with brown spots and bloodshot eyes. The other one is smaller, with twisted gray tufts sprouting out all over, even out of its ears. I start to reach my hand into the cage.

"Don't touch. The gray one bites strangers." Andrew comes over to me and puts his arms around me from the back.

I look around the room. There are several Japanese posters on the wall. "You don't seem like you'd be into anime," I say.

"Mmm," he mutters, and kisses my neck, breathes into my hair. "I've been wanting to touch you all night." His breath is hot. The fat spotted rabbit pierces me with its red eyes. I suddenly think of this mug Viv has with bunnies drawn all over it, every which way in piles of bunny mass. She calls it the "humping bunny" mug. Some BF gave it to her.

Andrew turns me around so we are facing, and he finds my lips.

This is it. This is what I want. Someone to have sex with. This could be the night. But I don't kiss back. Instead I go limp. I can't seem to move my body.

He keeps kissing and moves his lips down my neck. Does this feel good? I'm not sure. I can't feel anything but his hot breath. I keep hearing Toad, Viv, Josh, Elwood the Shrink, and Mrs. V.O. in my head. Can't they leave me alone to have sex in peace?

Andrew has his hands inside my sweater, rubbing up and down my back. He moves them around to my front and jiggles my breasts. "Sweet," he mutters.

I know I should put my arms around him, kiss back, make a sound, react somehow, but I can't. I liked talking to him more than this. I want to know more about him. I want to ask him more about his life traveling with his gypsy family. I want to tell him I am not a college student majoring in philosophy. That I live three blocks away with my mother who has a young BF, soon to be husband.

He puts my hand on his crotch and rubs it back and forth with his hand, trying to get me to stroke him. I can feel him hard through his pants. I pull away. I am not ready for this.

His breath is faster now, and he doesn't seem to notice or care that I am not doing anything. I could be anyone, anything. I could be a blow-up doll he is caressing for all he notices. This thought makes me want to scream, "I am here, dammit!"

"Let's take this off," he says. He starts to pull my sweater over my head, and finally I react.

"Wait." I move my hand to stop his. He backs off. Finally noticing.

"What's wrong? I thought you were into me. I thought we had a connection."

"We do," I say. "At least, I think so. I don't know. Maybe not. How do I know? I don't even know you."

"I just told you my life story," he says. His hands are on my shoulders, but his touch is light. I think he is genuinely surprised. I guess I am too.

"I thought I could do it, but I can't," I say.

He takes his hands away and sighs.

"It's late." I look at my watch and it *is* late. Almost one a.m. "I should go."

He is perplexed. Of course he is. He thought I was a sure thing, and here I am unsure.

"Okay." His voice is distant. There is no flirtation in it.

"You can call me." I look around the desk for something to write on. I grab a Post-it and write my number. "You can call tomorrow. Maybe we can get together and do something. Go for a bike ride. It's supposed to be a nice day."

"Sure," he says.

I stick the Post-it on the rabbit cage. Both rabbits give me a surly look. The gray one curls its mouth back.

"It was nice meeting you," I say, backing out the door. "Call me tomorrow." I know I sound desperate, but I don't want to leave him, or me, without any hope. I want to leave the option open. He could be the one, but I need to make sure.

Before he has a chance to say anything else I close the door, breathing a huge sigh of relief. I hadn't realized how stifling it was in his room.

I run home with the wind pushing against tears. Me. Alone. In the middle of the night. I lost my chance. I may never get another. I am such a wimp. He wanted me. He was nice. I liked him. And here I am alone. Still.

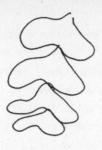

Andrew's Story

All of Sunday goes by and Andrew does not call. I check my phone a thousand times. Several times I think it is ringing, but it is only some other noise—a bird, a song, a car.

Finally at seven o'clock I ride my bike over to Smith House. I will tell him the truth. If we had anything last night or if it is going to become anything, he will understand. I will apologize, he will apologize, and all will be fine.

Suddenly I do want to kiss him. I want his arms around me. I want to feel him. I want to explore him. I am okay now. I am ready. Maybe it was the pot that made me nervous. I don't want my first time to be when I am stoned. I want to be present. I will explain all this and we will have sex tonight. I have a condom in my pocket. We will have comfortable, caring, loving, body-exploring, mind-numbing sex. I am excited by the time I arrive at Smith House.

I run up the stairs, find his room, and knock. I have it all planned out how I will hug him the minute he opens the door.

I knock again and hear some shuffling.

"Hang on," a voice calls. Not his voice. A female voice. Shit. He's found someone else. I hadn't planned for this.

The door opens and the girl with the pigtails from the party last night is there. Her pigtails are disheveled and she is wearing a bathrobe. Seven p.m. on a Sunday. Have they been in bed all day?

"Yeah, what?" she asks, sounding pissed that she has to be up at all.

"Uuhhh," I stammer. I don't know what to say now.

"I recognize you from last night," she says. "You left with Andrew."

"Um, is he here?" I still think I can explain things, or maybe he can explain things. The least he can do now is explain things to me. Was I just chopped liver to him after all? This is why he didn't call all day. He found someone else. Well, you snooze, you lose. I guess I lost.

The girl snorts a laugh. More like a guffaw. "He told you this was his room?"

I nod.

She shakes her head. "He told you he went to school here?"

I nod.

"Well. He lied. Andrew went home this morning."

My face makes the question I dare not ask.

She goes on. "He's my little brother. He comes to visit every once in a while and pretends he's a big college student. Ha! In his dreams. He still has two years to go. That kid can lie like a rug!"

"But, living in the RV with his siblings who have all gone to jail . . . being gypsies . . ."

"He told you that? Man, that little twerp. We have a perfectly nice family in New Hampshire. He's lived there his entire life. He has one sister—me."

I turn to leave. "Thanks," I mumble.

Her face gets softer. "Hey, I'm sorry. Did you . . . you know, go all the way?"

I shake my head.

"Well, that's good then. He's too young to be sleeping with college girls. You a freshman?"

I shake my head again, then nod it, but don't say anything. She doesn't pressure for an answer. I gaze into her room from the doorway. The rabbits glare at me. I notice the Post-it with my number is gone. Was it thrown away, did it lose its stickiness and fall to the bottom of the rabbit cage, or did he actually take it? I may never know.

"There are plenty of cuter and more mature guys here. Well, cuter, anyway." She laughs at her own joke. Then catches herself and says, "Sorry," again.

I ride home feeling crummy and used. We hadn't done anything. I lied to him too, so we should be even.

The thing is, I wanted another chance. I did want to talk to him more. I did want to tell him the truth. I did want to kiss him, to have him kiss me again.

I decide to believe that he took my number and all I have to do is wait for him to eventually use it. I can wait. Maybe.

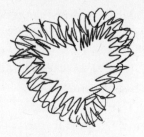

College Sendoff

Sometime in February I manage to fill out all the forms for my college applications and rewrite the personal essay half a dozen times before I am satisfied. I make two copies, write out two checks for the application fee, and slip them into the appropriate envelopes. One school I want to go to and one backup, just because.

Tessa and I walk to the end of the street and I slide both envelopes down the mailbox slot. I give the box a ceremonial pat and then I give one to Tessa.

"My ticket out of here," I say to her. "Let's hope it works. Plan B isn't as solid." I don't exactly have a Plan B except to go somewhere, Boston, maybe, and get a job and an apartment.

Tessa gives me a sad look.

"I'll miss you too, girl, but I have to do this. I have to go. They don't allow dogs at college. I don't know why. Maybe after a year in the dorm I'll get a place off-campus and bring you."

Tessa wags her tail, already excited at this thought.

"In the meantime, Viv will take you out, and I'll make sure to have Toad come by every day after school, just in case."

This makes Tessa even more excited and her tail wags uncontrollably. We race back home.

My Body

The more I run, the more I am aware of shifts in my body. My legs are getting stronger. My calves and hamstrings are taut. I can run all the way around the bay now without walking, plus there and back. That's five miles. When I go up and down stairs my muscles hurt a little. I like this feeling—they are being used. I stand straighter and keep my shoulders pulled back.

I have been really into my body lately. Looking at it, touching it, wearing underwear that makes me feel sexy. I want other people to touch me too. Admire me. Feel me. I feel power in my body. Too bad no one is around to take advantage of me. If only I had someone to touch me, I'd be all right. Someone to tell me it's okay. That nothing is my fault. There must be something in me that automatically repulses people.

Driving with Toad

Even though I am running all the time now, sticking to my four-times-a-week schedule and up to six miles, it feels like other things are getting worse. I've never felt this lonely. Andrew never called and probably never will. I can barely look at Josh anymore. I don't think he has asked Viv to marry him yet. Apple started seeing Chip—she told him the truth and he didn't care at all.

Tina is studying all the time now for her finals, but one night she manages to make eggplant lasagna for supper and Viv invites Josh and Sandra over for a family meal. Sandra is taking a separation from her husband in Connecticut and has temporarily moved back.

Everyone is laughing and joking except me.

"Have you got any more of that stuff, Viv?" Sandra asks.

Viv glances at me and gives a warning sign to Sandra.

"What?" Sandra says. "She knows you have dope. She probably smokes it herself."

Viv puts her hand on my shoulder like I am a little kid.

I shove her hand away. "Stop it!" I yell.

Viv raises both arms as if she's been caught. The others laugh. Josh says something about the food and they go back to eating as though nothing happened.

I excuse myself and go upstairs to call Toad. I haven't talked to him in a while, and suddenly I miss him.

"Hi, Lo," he answers.

"Hey!" I shout, happy to hear his voice. "You're there."

"Yeah," he says.

"Do you want to come over? I'll go for a drive with you. Anywhere you want to go."

Toad loves joy riding. He can drive for hours along back roads, down to the city, with the music cranked. He says driving is like meditating for him. I can't even imagine.

"What's wrong?" he asks.

"Nothing," I say, too fast to be believable. "Can't I just want to go for a drive with you?"

"I don't know, Lopi. You never call anymore. I hear you're smoking and drinking and sleeping around and suddenly you want to go for a ride? I don't know you anymore."

"I miss you," I say.

Toad sighs and goes quiet. He can never stay mad for long.

I bite my lip. "I'm sorry I haven't called in a while. But you can call me too, you know."

"I've been dealing with my own stuff."

"Well, let's go and you can tell me all about it."

He sighs again, but I know I have him. "Okay," he says. "I'll be there in twenty."

"Don't come in," I say. "Honk and I'll meet you out front."

When I hear the car horn, I fly down the stairs. "I'm going out with Toad!" I yell to the jovial voices in the kitchen. I'm out the door before I hear a response.

I give Toad a kiss on the cheek and say, "You're a doll."

"Humph." He's still trying to be mad, but I can see a smile under his grumpy pout. "Where do you want to go, Your Majesty?" he asks.

"I don't care. Just drive."

He turns onto the highway. I turn on the radio and find a song worth listening to, open the window, and wave my arm in the wind. The Mustang shakes when she goes over sixty.

Toad doesn't say anything. Just stares at the road and drives. I look at him—he is wearing a T-shirt and his upper arm tenses as he holds the wheel. He's still gangly, but he looks strong.

I squeeze his muscle. "Have you been working out?" I tease.

He smiles. "'Bout time you noticed."

"I am capable of noticing some things."

"I'll bet." He smirks. "So what has been going on? Why the call tonight?"

"Oh, Viv and Josh are at it again. I can't stand all their entertaining. They treat me like some ignorant infant."

"There's more."

"What do you mean?" I say.

"You haven't been providing me with the up-to-date Lopi report. I count on you for my entertainment, you know. There must be something going on, and I bet it involves S-E-X." His voice gets lower all of a sudden. "You haven't been in the Hole, have you?"

Almost always when I am in the Hole, I manage to call Toad, or he figures it out by my lack of calling and showering. He makes an effort to bring me out—invites me somewhere or brings me cookies or tells me to get some exercise. Occasionally it works.

"I haven't been in the Hole for months," I say.

"You met someone?" Toad asks.

"Well, sort of," I start.

"I knew it!" Toad lets his breath out. "Who?"

"It's nothing, really." I tell him about the frat party with Apple. I tell him about smoking pot and Andrew bringing me water, and how Andrew and I really connected. I tell him about the rabbits. But I don't tell him everything. I don't tell him that Andrew lied and is not actually a college student. I don't tell him about the next day and his sister with the pigtails. And I definitely don't tell him that I told Apple he and I had slept together.

"So, did you do the down and dirty? Let me look at you." Toad scrutinizes my face.

"No. I chickened out. Again."

A look of relief passes through Toad's eyes. "Yeah, I can tell. You look the same."

"You think I'm going to look different after I have sex? You think you'll be able to tell?"

"Yeah, I do."

Sometimes Toad thinks he knows all there is to know about me. Sometimes I like this; sometimes, like now, I'm not so sure.

"So you made out and left, and he hasn't called," Toad recaps. "Are you surprised? The guy didn't get lucky. Why would he try for a second time? That's just begging for rejection. Rejected once is an honest misread, rejected twice spells loser, or a glutton for punishment."

"What's wrong with me, Toad?"

"You suffer from lack of affection, no male role models. You think sex is the answer to love. You're craving the male attention you never got as a child. Every boy you meet is potential father-love."

"Seriously, Toad."

"You asked."

"Father-love, my foot."

"Hey, pay some shrink a hundred bucks to give you the same answer. You don't need me."

"I'll always need you, Toad."

He gives me a long look. Serious now. "You may not."

"What do you mean? Of course I will. We're bonded by childhood."

"I may not always be available, you know."

"Oh, pshaw. Where are you going?"

"You never know . . . you just never know," he says, all secretive.

"We'll always love each other," I say. "You and me. Frog and Toad." I put my hand on his shoulder, tickle his neck.

He waves it off as if it's a gnat. "That was a stupid game we played as kids. We're not kids anymore. You'll find some great lover, and me . . . well, maybe I will too."

"Are you still mad at me for deciding to get out of the prison early?"

"It doesn't help," he says, "you leaving me all alone."

"You'll find some great girl, Toad. You'll forget all about me." I am saying this, but the last thing I want is for Toad to forget me.

"Which reminds me . . . what did you say to your friend Apple? She seems to think I want to go out with her."

"Don't you? She's cute. She'd do it with you, except I think you're too late. She found a boyfriend. If you keep working out, though, all the girls are gonna drool all over you."

"Maybe I don't want all the girls to drool."

The way he says this makes me look at him carefully. In the dark glow of the streetlamps he looks soft and almost angelic. "Does this mean you like boys? I knew it!" I pretend this makes me happy, but I can't help but feel a slight twinge of disappointment and I'm not sure why.

"Just because I don't want girls to drool doesn't mean that I am automatically gay, you know?"

"I know," I say. There is silence for a minute, and then I say, "So, you're not gay?"

"No. At least, I don't get erections when I think of guys."

"But you think of guys?"

"Jeez, Lopi, what do you want, for me to be gay? Would that make you happy?"

"I don't care what you are," I say, not meaning it. "Sometimes I wish *I* could be gay. It seems like it would be easier to find someone of your own gender to sleep with. At least then all their parts wouldn't be so strange."

Toad smiles. "Yeah. Mrs. V.O. would love you. You could join LGBTQF."

"Anybody can. F is for friends," I remind him. "How come you don't want to have sex?" I ask.

"I didn't say that. I just don't want it with any random person. I want to be in love."

Like me, I think. *I want to be in love too.* I look at him and he looks different. It's not just that he looks stronger and more mature. I start to think maybe I already do love Toad more than as a friend, but I chase that thought away and keep my stiff exterior. "You are such a hopeless romantic," I say. I turn the music up. "This is a great song," I shout.

Toad nods and drives. We drive and drive and drive.

When we get back to my house, Sandra's car is gone. Josh's is still there. The lights are off except for Viv's upstairs.

Toad lets the car idle. "I don't want to go in," I say. "Can I stay at your house tonight?" I am shocked that I ask this question, not sure what kind of answer I want. Toad looks shocked too, and a little disappointed.

I used to stay at Toad's. After the accident I stayed there for a few weeks so Viv could grieve and recover. Toad had his own room with a bunk bed, and we used to tickle-fight to see who would win top bunk. I always won, but I think sometimes Toad let me. In middle school I stayed with him whenever Viv went on one of her "special" weekend-away trips with her BF. She'd drop me off at the Zebowskis'.

123

Mrs. Z. never refused me. She has three boys, Toad and the twins, who are ten, and I think she thinks of me as a surrogate daughter.

The last time I stayed for a full sleepover, Toad had his futon mattress on the floor. We moved another mattress in and made a huge room-size bed. There was plenty of room to stay far away from each other, but somehow by morning we had both migrated to the middle, snug against each other. It was a nice feeling. But that was three years ago.

"I don't want to go home yet," I explain. "Josh is staying over. I hate hearing them."

"You're going to have to get used to that. Isn't he going to be moving in once they're married?"

I groan. "That's only if they last that long. Besides, I don't think he's even asked her yet."

"It's been almost a year. That's a record for Viv, isn't it?"

"Don't remind me."

"What's wrong with Josh? Besides that he's younger than your mom, and that you made a fool of yourself by trying to make a pass at him. Your mom seems genuinely happier and she's leaving you alone more."

There are times when I regret telling Toad every single thing, which is exactly why I had to be careful about Andrew.

"Shut up, Toad."

"Oh, did I hit a tender spot?"

"Just shut up, okay?"

He does.

"So, can we go to your place?"

He shakes his head. "I don't think it's such a good idea."

"But why?"

"It's not that simple, Lopi. We're not little kids anymore. We can't have sleepovers. There's nowhere for you to sleep—we don't have a guest room."

"We can put the extra mattress on your floor. Make the really big bed."

"You can't stay with me," he says.

"Why not?" Now I do sound like a little kid. "I don't understand. We're friends. I'm not going to try to sleep with you." In my head, though, I am not sure about this.

"You just can't." He says this with a finality I've never heard from him before.

I open the door and get out.

"Bye, then," I say.

"Lopi." I hear agony in his voice, a desire to make things good between us, but I don't give him the chance.

"Thanks for nothing," I say, and slam the door shut.

If I Were to Die

These are things I would miss if I were to die:

1. Tessa

2. Talking to Toad

3. The memory of my mother when she used to sing to me.

That's all I can think of. That's not really much. Mrs. V.O. would probably miss me, but she's a teacher, so she's used to her students leaving. I'm sure none of them comes back to say hi, or writes. Just for the record, I would. And Viv of course would be devastated to lose another child—it would be a trauma to her, for sure, and she'd need a lot of comfort. Good thing she has Josh.

Another Date with
Elwood the Shrink

"Do you think I seek male attention because my father left when I was six?" I ask in my imaginary conversation with Elwood the Shrink.

"Is that what you think?"

"It's a theory. It makes sense, though, right? Sexual issues are because of the father. Eating issues are because of the mother. I don't have an eating disorder, so it must be my father."

"Parents are not always to blame for everything."

"They're not?"

"Some believe that a person's makeup is preconditioned. Innate rather than learned. People are born a certain way, perhaps due to genetics. Environment may or may not exaggerate such conditions."

"But even if it's genetic and not due to environment, it's still the parents' genetics, right?"

"Yes, though genetics is not something we can change or control. Actions and circumstances are."

"Not unless your actions are that way due to your

genetics," I counter. "Some people are just born evil."

"Let's go back to your original question. I think it's a good one. Why do you think your father left?"

"He couldn't live with Viv. I don't blame him. I can't either." I do not say the real reason my father left.

"What about your brother?"

I go blank. I try to numb my mind—clear it from the images that start to take over. This is all in my head, I tell myself. I don't have to think about this. But I do. I see Adam in his swimsuit. Adam lying on the driveway, his tiny body empty of life. My mother's look of terror. An ambulance. A hospital. A funeral. It's all too much to remember, so I think of nothing but the word *blank*. *Blank, blank, blank*. I repeat it over and over until my mind *is* blank.

"Lopi?"

"I don't want to talk about that."

"Okay. Another question, then. When was the last time you saw your father?"

I breathe. This is an easier question. "I don't know. Pretty much never. I hardly remember him."

"Yet you remember Adam?"

"Yes," I say. I see Adam clearly in my mind, but my father is all fuzzy.

"Do you think about death?"

"Sometimes. I wonder if there is an afterlife. Sometimes I think Adam came back as Tessa."

"Lopi, what do *you* want?"

"If I knew that I wouldn't need a shrink, would I?"

"You don't have a shrink. I'm only in your head."

128

"You're all I have," I say.

"Do you love Toad?"

"No!" I say too fast. "Toad is my friend. I could never lose him." Though I may have lost Toad anyway.

"Your mother has found someone she loves, someone special, someone who loves her too. It's possible."

"Not for me."

"Why do you think you are so unlovable?"

"You know why."

"Can you say it?"

"Because I ruin everything. Things are fine until I think something bad, and then it turns to shit."

"How can you change that?"

"I can find someone else. Move on. I don't need Toad. I would only end up ruining it like I do everything else. Or I can disappear."

Elwood the Shrink does not disagree.

Sex Story

When I was twelve, I wrote a story in my diary. It was really sexual.

It went something like this: A young teenage girl goes to a diner and meets a guy. He asks her if she needs a ride home and she says sure. They make out and he tries to go all the way. She says she's thirteen and then he kicks her out of the car and says she's too young and to come back in two years. It was a little more graphic than that, but basically that's the gist.

I imagine Elwood the Shrink having a heyday with this story. It's right up a shrink's alley. He would say it's interesting that there is violence to it and that it takes place in a car. But then, I suppose I am a violent person and I hate cars.

The boy doesn't rape her, he just gets pissed at her. She was the one who wanted it and initiated it, and ultimately she was rejected for being too young.

At the end of the story the guy drives away furiously,

car tires peeling on the gravel. The girl is left on the sidewalk with her panties literally in a bunch, feeling like she just ruined everything.

Ways to Die

1. Accident
2. Illness
3. Murder
4. Suicide
5. Old Age

Golden Boy

I ignore Toad, which is surprisingly easy to do, since he ignores me too. I take my own advice and am moving on to a new boy. It helps to have someone, something, to focus on. It keeps me going, distracts me from my own wallowing self. This time it is someone more likely. Charley, in Mrs. V.O.'s class. I think he may have eyes for me. The last several weeks he has been watching me. He is a pure golden boy. He has golden hair, golden skin, and a golden smile that shines all the way through his golden-flecked eyes. He's the boy everybody likes. He plays on the lacrosse team, gets honors in school, drinks and smokes enough to be social but not get in trouble. Girls fawn over him, guys want to be his best friend, teachers treat him with respect. He's the type that usually never notices me.

Until recently. Ever since Mrs. V.O. read my paper on existentialism out loud to the class he's been eyeing me. Today we are reading *The Stranger* out loud. I am to read first.

I start. "Maman died today. Or yesterday maybe, I don't

know. I got a telegram from the home: 'Mother deceased. Funeral tomorrow. Faithfully yours.' This doesn't mean anything. Maybe it was yesterday." I pause, glance around me. Charley is looking at me. Apple is looking at him, then at me, and winks.

Someone asks, "How can this guy care so little? I mean, his mother just died."

"He must have hated her," someone else says.

"How do you know it's a guy?" I ask.

"It's written by a guy."

"Plus, a girl wouldn't feel so . . . *nothing*. Only a guy can be so uncaring," this from Apple.

"Are we sure the character is uncaring?" Mrs. V.O. asks.

"Sure—he doesn't even know which day his mother died. He got the news in a telegram. He hardly even reacts."

"And it's in the first person, so we would know."

"Maybe this is the way he reacts," I say. "Maybe he is just removed and can't be all emotional yet. Is it a guy?"

"Let's read on," Mrs. V.O. says.

How *can* this guy be so nonchalant? I am almost jealous. I want to be that removed, uncaring. How much easier my whole life would have been if I didn't care what happened to Adam. If I didn't care if my own mother died.

As the next person reads I can feel Charley's golden eyes penetrating me. I glance at him just to be sure it is me he is looking at, and sure enough he flashes gleaming white teeth and gives me a half wave. Me.

I melt into my chair, the warmth of his goldenness spreading through my body and enveloping me like a hug.

It's as though the very things he chooses to look at turn to gold as well. Today I am the chosen thing. I am gold. This I can have feelings about.

The bell rings and I am aware of him standing up, gathering his books, walking toward the door. He is lingering, waiting for me. I should go up to him. But I don't move. He smiles and leaves.

I don't want to ruin this like I've ruined everything else. A golden boy might help me find some goodness in myself. I crave gold more than anything. I don't want to be so bad all the time. I really don't.

I vow to write him a note later. I can say it all in a note.

The Milk Line

I stay up late. It's after midnight and I am restless. When I am restless I like to organize. I start by cleaning my desk. I take everything off and dust it down. I love my desk. It's just a long piece of heavy plywood over two sets of drawers. I painted it dark green last year. The best thing about it is that it's big—it takes up almost the entire length of my wall—so I can fill up the space with piles of paper and stuff. At least then it looks like I am doing something. When it's all dusted I organize the piles. English homework goes in one pile, science in another. Math, history, and so forth. The books I'm not done reading I leave out, and the books I've finished go back on the shelf. Pens and pencils go in the humping bunny mug I took from the cupboard. I even line up my collection of sushi pencil erasers that Viv's BF last year brought back from Japantown in San Francisco.

When the desk is finally to my liking, I sit down and start writing a letter to Charley Golden Boy. I use the stationery I got for Christmas. It's very girly, with pink and purple flowers and curlicues around the edges. Sandra gave it to me.

Dear Charley, I start. *We don't really know each other, but we are in the same English class. I don't mean to be forward, but do you have a girlfriend?* I stop. I can't ask him that! I ball up the paper and toss it. I take out another piece of stationery and start again. *Dear Charley, Do you believe in love at first sight?* Stupid. I toss that one and take out a clean regular piece of paper, no flowers. *Charley, I have noticed you noticing me in English class. I think you are really interesting. At least, you have a nice smile. I think we could be friends if we had the chance to get to know each other better. What do you say?*

This might be okay. Though I don't know why I shake as I write it. It's hard to write what you mean. I figure the friends-first approach might work better than the I-want-to-jump-your-bones-right-now approach. Start slow, and who knows? I don't want to scare him away by being too honest.

I debate how to close it. *Love* is too much, *sincerely* is too formal, and just my name is too cold. I finally decide on *In hopes of new friendship, Lopi.* That sounds genuine. I fold it, put it in an envelope, and seal it before I change my mind. I write his name on the front and place the envelope in the middle of my clean desk. I'll put it in his locker tomorrow. What have I got to lose?

I am about to tape the letter to Charley's locker when

suddenly someone is behind me. "Hey," he says. I jump. It's him. I hadn't planned on this.

"Oh," I say, stalling.

"What are you doing?"

"Uh, nothing."

"Is that for me?" He points to the envelope with his name on it.

"No. I mean, yes. Here." I shove the envelope against his shirt, which also means I am touching him. I move my hand away fast and the envelope falls to the floor. He picks it up and starts to open it.

"It's nothing," I say, backing down the hall. "See you." I turn and run to class. I am so embarrassed. I just hope he sees beyond that and knows that I am not a complete idiot. He caught me by surprise. The only saving grace is that at least now he'll know for sure who I am, if he ever bothers to look at me again.

I suffer through Algebra 2, then Chemistry. Finally I head to lunch. I walk fast and don't run into Charley in the hall. Maybe he is going to avoid me now.

In the cafeteria I sit with Apple and a kid named Robert.

"What's new?" Apple says. "We haven't seen you for a while."

"I've been busy," I say.

"How's Josh?"

"Fine, I guess. He and Viv are away a lot."

"You should have a party," Robert says. "No supervision, and Apple says you've got a great house."

"Tina is there a lot," I say.

"Tina's cool." Apple met Tina a while ago and they hit

it off. Who wouldn't hit it off with Tina? "She wouldn't tell, would she? Besides, it's not as if Viv would care. She'd probably be upset that you had a party and she missed it."

Unfortunately, Apple is most likely right.

"I'll think about it," I say.

I keep looking around for Charley, and finally I see him sitting by himself in the far corner. This might be my only chance. I have to risk it.

"I have to go." I take my lunch and walk over to him.

"Hi," I say.

"Hey."

I stand awkwardly. "Did you get my letter?" I ask. Duh, of course he got it—I practically threw it at him. "I mean, did you read it?"

"Yeah," he says.

This is like pulling teeth, only slower and more painful. Why doesn't he just kill me now? Get it over with.

"Well, what do you think?" I pull up a chair but stay standing.

"Sit," he says. I do. "I thought what you wrote was . . ." Just then a friend of his comes over. A soccer jock named Burt. He sits down, glances at me for a millisecond, and starts talking to Charley about practice. I think about leaving but don't know how to leave gracefully, so I sit there pretending to listen.

Finally Charley stands up and announces, "I have to get a milk." Great, now he's going to leave me here with Burt. I am starting to wonder why I thought Charley was so golden in the first place.

"Come with," he says, motioning to me.

I jump up so fast the chair falls over. Burt laughs, but Charley waits quietly as I pick it up. I follow behind him to the milk line. He turns around and we look straight at each other. "Sorry about Burt," he says. "I wanted to talk to you in private."

I glance around at the kids in line. Not exactly private, but it's not like anyone is paying attention to us. He puts his hand on my shoulder. I start to get a little woozy.

"Your letter was nice," he starts.

Nice. Sure, but does he want to go out with me?

"And I think you're smart in English class and nice."

Again with the nice.

"Are you new this year?" he asks.

"I skipped junior year. I'm taking English Four so I can graduate this year."

"Oh, right—I heard about you. You're that smart kid who figured out how to get out early." He says this with approval, but then as an afterthought adds, "But you miss all the senior activities with your own class."

"I can do them with your class, if I want to," I say. Senior activities, as you can imagine, are not a high priority for me. In fact, missing them is yet another benefit to leaving school early. I've already missed a bunch, but there's still Senior Prank Day, Senior Skip Day, Senior Wear Shorts to School Day, Senior Flower Day, and the senior prom and all that goes with that. No thanks.

Charley smiles as if he is glad I am now able to do these things with his class. For a brief second I actually imagine that doing all those senior activities with him would make them fun. Maybe we'll even go to the prom together. I'll

140

wear a pretty pink dress and we'll eat at a Japanese restaurant before, and then snuggle against each other during the slow songs. We'll make love in a hotel room with a Jacuzzi in the bath.

"But I don't think that we can force anything, you know?" he says.

I nod, but I don't know.

"A friendship just happens. It can't be constructed."

So does that mean no, he doesn't want to get to know each other? He doesn't like me after all? Did I misread all those smiles? Wasn't that showing interest? All of a sudden I feel like such a dork.

He is waiting for me to say something. But what can I say? How else do things happen if we don't construct them? Finally, I say something along those lines. "How do you make a friendship if you don't construct it?"

He has an answer. "They evolve. You can't make it happen. It just happens. You know, like you start talking and then you find out you both like spaghetti Westerns or reading science fiction or something, and before you know it, you're friends."

"What are spaghetti Westerns?"

"They're these great old Western movies, really campy, made by some Italian director."

"That could be fun," I say. "I like old campy movies."

"Well, good. Maybe we can watch one sometime. See, that's a start."

I am so confused. Is he asking me out now? "So are we evolving?"

"Maybe—still too soon to tell. There has to be something in common. A common activity, or a regular meeting place."

I think about this. Is it true? Can you not become friends unless you see each other in the same place on a regular basis?

"We see each other in English every day," I say.

"That's true."

"And you smile at me." I am searching for a connection, a commonality, an excuse for us to evolve.

"All true," he says.

"Why?" I ask.

"Because you smile at me." He smiles now, his golden smile, which gives me courage, so I smile back. It's as if our smiles and our eyes, and maybe our hearts, say what our mouths cannot.

"Well, isn't that something we have in common? We both smile."

"Hmm." He looks as though he is contemplating this. Maybe we can force a friendship after all. There is a kind of quick-witted flirtation to our banter, strange as it is. I feel, dare I say, clever.

I go on. "It's hard to get to know someone when you only see them in class. Sometimes you have to make an effort. That's why I wrote. Should I not have written?"

"No, it was good you wrote. I'm glad you did. That's you being you."

Okay, here is my chance. I jump. "So maybe we should do something and see if we have anything else in common."

"Maybe you're right. We could see. We should go out."

I clap my hands together. I twirl with joy. I spin my arms around and shout *Yippee!* at the top of my lungs. In reality, I stand there and say, "Okay."

The lunch bell rings and we walk together. We have English next. We reach my locker and he stands next to me, waiting as I open it, switch my algebra book for Camus, and close it again. I am not looking at him, but I feel him standing there contemplating me.

I am still gold. In fact his golden energy gives me courage, strength, power, and a boldness I do not usually have. From somewhere else, somewhere not me for a second but from some beautiful golden girl, I say, "Do you want to go out this weekend?"

"Sure." He grins. I get to see those gleaming teeth again, and the smile of his eyes.

"Okay," I say. "Good."

We seal our golden fate with an exchange of numbers. All through English we give little glances, smiles, good feelings. I could like this guy, this sweet golden boy. We are going out this weekend.

Pure

"You will *never* in a million, zillion years guess who I am going out with this weekend." I catch up with Toad on the way home. I am so excited that I can easily pretend we didn't have a fight and that we are back to normal.

"Josh?" he guesses, knowing he's wrong and it will only annoy me.

"No."

"Andrew?"

"Who?" I pretend I don't remember that fiasco.

"You know, rabbit boy."

"Nope."

"Mr. Koch?"

"Get real. I told you you'd never guess."

"Who, then? Not yours truly? Have you decided to fall in love with me once and for all?"

I ignore that comment and pause for dramatic effect, then say, "Charley Golden Boy!"

"Oh, yeah. Everybody's favorite."

144

"He is beautiful. He's like a prince, a knight in golden armor."

"Yeah, whatever. I'm sure you will have beautiful children together."

I frown at his cynicism. "What's the gossip on him?" I ask.

"He's pure. Everyone likes him. He does no wrong."

"I mean, has he slept with anyone? What about that girl last year he was dating?"

"Christ, Lopi, you think he tells me these things? I've spoken maybe three words to the guy in my entire life."

"But you used to play lacrosse. What's the locker room talk?"

"Guys don't blab the way you girls seem to think we do. At least not Charley. Like I said, he's pure."

"I just wonder if *pure* means *virgin.*"

"I guess you'll find out," Toad says, and I can't help but smile at the thought.

Love

They say love makes people crazy. Maybe that's why Viv is crazy—she is always in love. They also say that love makes you see the world differently. That where everything once was gray and dull, love makes everything radiate with splendid color.

A girl who is truly in love leaves a trail of flowers growing in her footsteps. I keep checking for the flowers behind me, but all I see are the dead ants I've trampled.

Love is not so far from hate. Joy is not so far from pain. Sanity is not so far from madness. Good is not so far from evil. I am on the brink of all these things, teetering somewhere just in the middle, precariously balanced and constantly wobbling from one side to the other. One push in either direction and that's where I'll fall. Most days it feels far closer to the hate, pain, mad, evil side than to the other.

What Happens in the Car

Charley Golden Boy picks me up in his black Volkswagen Beetle on Saturday afternoon. We drive to the park and go for a walk.

"You know there's a stream down that hillside," he says. "Come see."

I follow him off the path, down a steep hill, and into the woods until we get to a trickle of water gurgling over rocks and pebbles. We sit on a mossy rock and poke sticks into the stream.

"It is pretty," I say. I toss a pebble and watch the ripples.

"You're pretty," he says.

I don't know what to say. No one has ever called me pretty before.

"I know what I said about not forcing stuff and all," he says, "but I like you. I don't know why. I like that you're so bold."

At the moment I am not feeling especially bold. Why must I always freeze up at the most opportune moments? It's like a curse.

Charley moves closer to me, takes my hand, and puts his other arm around me. "I would like to kiss you. Can I kiss you?"

I look at his golden lips and say, "I guess so. Sure."

We move heads together and find lips. He is soft and gentle, just like he looks. We kiss for a while and then start to swirl our tongues and kiss harder. Our teeth clack together a couple times. His puts his hands under my shirt, fumbles with my bra hook. I am reminded of Andrew, except that I am much more excited about this. I want his hands on me. I help him unhook my bra. He moves his head down and kisses my breasts, kneels and kisses my stomach. I hope there is no poison ivy around. I feel a tickle on my leg. It's not him. I shake my leg, reach down, and pick off a tick.

I hold it out on my fingertip. "You want this?" I say jokingly.

Charley laughs. "Gross. No, thanks. Nasty blood suckers."

I squeeze the tick between my nails, hopefully killing it, and flick it into the stream.

"I'm not sure it's safe to lie down here," I say.

"What makes you think we were going to lie down?"

"Oh, just the natural progression of things."

"Do you want to go back to the car?" he asks.

The car would not be my first choice, but seeing as there is no other and I want to keep doing this, I nod.

We sit in the car for a minute. He turns on the CD player

and finds a song. "Now, where were we?" He leans over and we start kissing again.

"Kissing is nice," I say. Is this my fantasy come true? Is this what I couldn't have with anyone else?

"Mmm," he says.

"Not enough kissing in the world."

"Mmm," he says.

He is kissing my neck, fondling my breasts. His hands keep going down, and they reach the waist of my jeans, go around, and grab my butt. He climbs on top of me, moving up and down. Moaning soft moans. He stops kissing and breathes in my ear. It's hot. I put my arms around his back since I'm not sure what else to do. Should I unzip him, stroke him? He says my name and moves faster. I am smooshed underneath his weight. His hands are everywhere and then he starts touching himself, unzipping his own jeans. The tenderness is gone and he seems to have disappeared. I look at his face. His eyes are closed, his cheeks are red, there is a thin line of sweat next to his ear. He doesn't look like Charley Golden Boy anymore. And then just as suddenly as the tender kisses stopped, his moaning stops and he is still, except for his breathing and his heart beating a million times a minute.

He rolls off me and back to the driver's seat. The same song is playing. He turns it up. I pull my shirt down. I guess it's over.

I touch his shoulder and he turns to look at me.

"Are you okay?" he asks.

"Yeah," I say.

"I like you, Lopi," he says.

Now it is my turn to say "Mmm."

He starts the car and we drive back. When he drops me off, he kisses me on the cheek.

"I had a nice time," he says.

I should say I had a nice time too, but I don't.

"I'll see you in school," he says.

"Yeah, in English." I have to remind myself how I know him. Who he is. "See you Monday."

I get out and close the door. I have an image of the story I wrote when I was twelve. But this is different, I tell myself. Charley is sweet; he doesn't peel out angrily. He waves his hand as he pulls slowly forward and drives into the evening.

Going Out

In sixth grade when all four elementary schools converged into one middle school people fell in and out of love all the time. One day you'd get a note or a whisper that so-and-so wanted to "go with you." If you liked the person you said yes, and then you'd be going together. This meant you'd smile in the halls, sit at the same table at lunch, talk on the phone in the evenings, and maybe go for a bike ride or see a movie on the weekend. A little kissing maybe, but that totally depended on the bravery of both involved. This would go on for a day, a week, in rare cases a month, until one of you decided to break up—either because you got wind that someone else was interested in going with you or you genuinely wanted to be single for a while. By the next day, chances were you'd get another invitation from someone else.

That's how it was until high school, when all of a sudden people stopped going together and started sleeping together. Just like that. Instead of going out they'd be staying in. At least that was the general impression. I doubt all that much of it is true—but one thing about high school is that it runs mostly on whatever a few key people say.

I had my heyday in sixth grade. I went with at least five boys during the year. Then it stopped. I didn't see the sense anymore in going out when we didn't ever actually go anywhere, and besides that, the boys stopped asking me. Now am I dating Charley? I don't even know if we had sex. I mean I know *I* didn't have sex, but did he? I liked kissing him, but why? And why are there always more questions than answers? I really, really want to see a therapist. Elwood the Shrink cannot help. I don't want to be depressed. I still want to go to college, but I can't seem to get myself out of this funk. When something good barely begins to happen, a big gray cloud of confusion swallows it. Who will ever save me? How will I ever be good enough for someone pure like Charley?

The Dinner

Since Charley and I maybe are going out now, I invite him over for dinner. At least I know where he lives and how old he is, that he's not dating my mother and not lying to me. That's a step in the right direction.

I invite him on a night I know everyone will be out. Tina suggested I make lasagna, saying it was a safe guys' dish — hearty, yet fancier than pasta, with nothing to give you bad breath. It was a little more complicated than I'd expected, cooking the flat noodles and then layering them with meat and cheese.

I run upstairs to shower and dress, then set the table with some fresh daffodils in honor of spring.

Six o'clock exactly and he knocks on the door.

"Hey," he says.

"Hey, yourself."

"You look nice."

I'm not wearing anything special, jeans and a white shirt, though it took me an hour to choose it. "Thanks."

"It smells good in here. Did you cook?"

I nod.

"Wow, I thought we'd get a pizza or something."

"I made lasagna. I hope it came out okay. It's the first time I've made it." I'd been planning to fool him into thinking I was a great chef, but the truth just came out.

"Well, it smells great. My mom never cooks. Not since she got divorced, anyway."

"My mom doesn't cook either, but we have this college student living with us and she's a great cook—she gave me this recipe."

He follows me into the living room while I put on some music. Tessa follows him around. He ignores her. I can see him taking everything in. The funky art, all the knick-knacks Viv has around. When he gets to the nude sculpture on the mantel he turns away, embarrassed. "My mom took a sculpture class last year and did that," I explain. "She's always taking some class and making things. That's a lot of what's in the house. And she collects things. She can't throw anything away. And she's always doing something new. Last month she took swing lessons and now can't stop playing swing music and dancing all the time. Before that she was into Zen meditation. I thought that might get her to get rid of some stuff, but it didn't." I stop myself. Why am I talking about my mother? I don't want to talk about Viv.

Charley laughs. "Wow, she must be interesting."

"Mmm." I think of something to change the subject. "What are you going to do your final paper on for Mrs. V.O.?"

He picks up one of the mini flower vases Viv made in a

154

pottery class and rubs it between his thumb and forefinger. "I was thinking of doing it on good and evil."

"Me too! Do you think people have parts of both in them, like Steinbeck says?" I can't imagine Charley Golden Boy having any evil in him. Even Toad says he's pure. But then I think of him in the car and I wonder if there's something else to him after all.

He puts the vase down. "I think we're born with both and can go either way."

"Yes!" I say excited. "But is it due to our environment or to something beyond our control? Say you're going in the good direction but then something happens that's evil. Can that make you evil?"

He thinks about this. "I guess it depends on what it is that happens, along with the makeup of your chemistry. I mean, why are some people able and even willing to kill and others could never harm a fly?"

"Sometimes it's brainwashing or political. Like suicide bombers. They actually believe they are doing the right thing." I am charged by our conversation. I want to keep talking, but just as I am about to say something else the front door opens and Viv hollers out a booming hello.

Charley's eyes widen. Viv has big presence.

"Well, hello there!" she says when she sees Charley in the living room. "Lopi didn't tell me we were having company. I'm Vivian, the mother, though I was really young when I had Penelope, so I hardly feel like a mother. Who are you?" She takes Charley's hand and holds it.

"Charley," she repeats when he says his name. "Delighted. It's so nice to meet some of Lopi's friends.

155

She always keeps me out of the loop."

Suddenly everything is ruined. I have nothing left to say, the charge is gone, and Viv takes over.

"It smells like something delicious is going on in the kitchen. It's a good thing my class was canceled. I'm starving. Are you old enough to have a glass of wine, Charley? Shall we open a bottle?"

Charley shrugs and says, "Sure." He follows her into the kitchen. I follow him. "You sure have a great house, Mrs. Yeager."

"Oh, no you don't, don't you dare do that. No one is allowed to call me Mrs. I have not been a Mrs. for years, and when I was I couldn't stand it either. It's Vivian, Charley. Or Viv."

"Vivian," Charley says. "Lopi says you made a lot of this stuff yourself. I really like the sculpture."

"Thank you, Charley. The female body is so curvy and elegant. Much more artistically interesting than the male. Wouldn't you agree?"

Charley laughs sheepishly and nods.

"The male body has some useful appendages though," Viv says.

I turn absolutely red. Charley does too.

The dinner goes in a similar painful manner. Viv talks nonstop. At one point she even touches Charley on the back of the hand. To his credit he moves his hand away fast.

"Now, tell me something, Charley. You're a friend of my daughter's. She never tells me anything. What's she like in school?"

Charley looks at me. "I don't know," he says. "You could ask her."

I smile a thank-you at him.

"Oh, but she doesn't say. I mean, I know she's smart, but I don't know what she's like—she's so secretive. Are all teenagers like that with their parents? Do you have secrets from your mother, Charley? You seem like such a clean-cut boy. I bet you tell your mother everything. But then, mothers and their sons have a special bond, don't they? No comparison or competition between them—just pure love."

"Viv," I say. I am starting to get really annoyed. I mean, how can she be so insensitive? "Maybe he doesn't want to talk about this."

"I'm just asking. I don't mean to make you uncomfortable, dear." She puts her hand on Charley's shoulder. "I'm just naturally curious."

All I can think is what a fake act this is. I hate her now more than maybe ever in my entire life.

"It's okay, Mrs. . . . Vivian. Actually, my mother's been really busy lately with a new job. My parents just got divorced."

This sends Viv into another rant about marriage and divorce.

When we are done eating, I mention to Charley that it might be time for him to go home.

"Oh, right. I do need to get home—it's late and it's a school night."

He says goodbye to Viv and thanks me for dinner. "It was great lasagna, Lopi."

"I'll walk you out," I say without looking at Viv. I dread a comment from her, but she refrains.

Instead she hugs Charley and says, "Really great to meet you, Charley. Come back anytime. Our door is always open. You'll have to come for one of Tina's dinners, and meet Josh too. We'll have you over for a proper Yeager meal."

When we are in the driveway next to his car I say, "I'm sorry."

"You're mother is a trip," he says. "I had fun."

I sigh. Perhaps I have lost this one too.

Charley takes my hand. "But next time let's do something just you and me. Maybe go somewhere else. I still want to get to know you better." He leans over and we kiss softly.

I watch him drive away. *Okay*, I think. *Not the most perfect night, but that was a* near *perfect kiss.*

"Sweet boy," Viv says as soon as I enter the house. "That one's a keeper. And cute as the dickens too. If he were a little older . . ."

Rage and anger bubbles up in me. I let it out. "I can't believe you did that!"

"What?"

"You know! What you always do! Take over."

"I wasn't taking over, honey. We were having a family dinner. I was just getting to know your friends."

"You have no right! You were flirting with him, right there in front of me!"

"I'm just being me—that's how I am. Besides, I've seen you flirt with Josh."

I am silenced, but Viv isn't. "Your Charley's got such a strong, lanky young body. "

"I hate you!" I shout. How dare she be so clueless and selfish. "I absolutely hate you!"

I have never said these words to her before. In fact, it seems most of this year I've hardly said anything to her. I don't know if she even knows that my hate is possible—that's how much she is in denial. Her face crumbles.

I go on: "My whole life, ever since Adam, you treat me like I'm not even here, like you don't care, and now you try to steal my boyfriend!" I am so riled up, I don't even realize I call Charley my boyfriend until after it comes out, but it doesn't matter. That's the least of it. The mention of Adam silences her.

I run up to my room. I pack a bag.

"Where are you going?" Viv asks on my way out the door. She has the phone in her hand, about to make a call. Josh, no doubt, so she can go cry to him, tell him what a mean and horrible daughter I am, and get some comfort.

"I'm going out. I can't be around you anymore. You make me sick." I am being mean and horrible, but I can't help it. I can't stop myself. "You're not a normal mother. You're hardly a mother at all. You never have been. You don't deserve me. You don't even want me. So I'm making your dreams come true. I'm leaving! I just wish I could get away even sooner, get away from you forever!"

I slam the door and hop on my bike, pedaling so fast, I almost topple over. I am not sure where I am going. I bike past Toad's. His bedroom light is on, but I don't stop. He doesn't want me. I bike all the way to Charley's. I am winded and sweating even though the night air is cool.

Charley lets me in and hugs me—doesn't ask anything, just hugs me.

"Please, can I sleep with you tonight?" I ask. Charley sneaks me down to his basement room and we crawl into his bed.

Strike Three

I am lying next to Charley. He has a private room in the basement, so it's easy to be there unnoticed. We ended up smoking a little pot and then most of our clothes came off. We've been making out and getting all hot and heavy. This is the best cure for anger I've ever had.

Now we are quiet, just looking at each other. I run my hand down the length of his golden arm.

"Pinch me," I say.

"You're not into pain, are you?" He laughs, with a hint of unease.

"No, no. I just don't believe this is real. I mean, one minute I'm screaming at my mother and the next I am here with you, practically naked."

"It's real," he says, and gives me a slight pinch on the forearm.

"Ow!" I pretend it really hurt and whop him with a pillow.

We start to kiss again and I forget everything except how

wonderful it is to be here. I reach under the covers to feel him, but he gently takes my hand away.

"Lopi," he says, "can we talk a minute?"

"You don't want to do this?" I panic that I've done something wrong, something he didn't like and he's going to kick me out.

"I'm not sure," he says. "You'll have to show me your tricks."

I squint at him. "Huh?"

"You know, last time . . . I came so fast. That was my first time with anyone. Like that."

"It's okay," I say quickly.

"I'm sorry," he says.

"It's okay," I say again. Somehow his admission takes my breath away. I want to say, *me too, this is my first time too,* but I can't quite. I'm still not exactly sure I want to do this with Charley.

"You must think I'm some inexperienced dolt," he says. "You're so comfortable, it's so easy for you. I bet you've done this a million times before—you have such a sophisticated life."

I laugh. "I have an active fantasy life, sure. But . . ." I pause. "I've never actually done it either." It feels surprisingly good to say this. I breathe easier and flash a smile.

"Really?" Charley sits up and stares at me, as though I've let him down somehow. My stomach starts to twist in a knot. "I thought you've done it a ton," he says. "That's what Apple said."

I jolt up. "What?" I say too loud. I cross my hands over my bare breasts, suddenly ashamed. "What?" I say again.

162

"I . . . uh . . . she said . . ." Charley stammers, trying to explain.

I find my bra, then my shirt, and start to dress. "Did she say I would do it with you? Is that why you asked me out?"

"No, that's not the only reason. I like you, Lopi. I mean, I do." He touches my arm where he pinched me. "I thought you could show me a few things."

I pull my arm back. "Well, I can't," I say. "You picked the wrong person."

"Can't we just fool around anyway?" he asks. "I like kissing you."

I snort at the absurdity. "I don't think so. I don't think I'm the one for you. I'm sorry, Charley."

I leave and get back on my bike. If I weren't so upset I could almost laugh at this. A part of me is relieved to have an excuse to leave. I head back home, where the driveway is empty of cars. Viv must have gone to Josh's. I crawl into my own bed with my sweet dog.

Josh, Andrew, Charley. Three strikes and I'm out.

The Fish

I hear Tina leave early in the morning, and when I finally stumble downstairs to let Tessa out I notice the note from Viv posted on the refrigerator. *Away for the weekend.*

I go upstairs and sit on my bed. My room is becoming a mess. I glance at the copy of *The Stranger*. That character just goes through the motions of life, waiting it out until his own death. I wonder if I could do that. Good or bad, nothing seems to matter. Nothing ever works out. Maybe it's time to just give up. I miss Toad.

I go over to my fishbowl and dip my hand in. I let the George the Twelfth circle around it a few times. I grab him and pull him out of the water. I close my hand around his tiny, slippery body. George the Twelfth squirms and tickles my palm. I open my hand and watch the golden belly heave in and out as he gasps for a way to breathe.

I could squish you dead, I think. I close my fingers around the fish again and squeeze. I open my hand. His belly is heaving faster now.

"That's right," I whisper, "be scared."

I squeeze harder and longer this time. I open my hand again. George the Twelfth looks straight at me with bulging eyes, as if pleading, begging for his life.

What am I doing? Am I a murderer now? I gently place George the Twelfth back in the bowl and he swims to the plastic plant and hovers in its tendrils, regaining his strength.

Back in the Hole

I stay in bed all the next day. I get up only to let Tessa out. I am not sick, but I can't do anything. I am sinking into the Hole for no reason other than nothing makes sense anymore. No one loves me and I am pining like a lonely idiot. Last night I had a nightmare in which I was driving and I saw Adam behind me, waving and smiling, and then he crumbled to the ground. I woke up in a cold sweat.

Viv might actually get married. She could have a whole new life. She could even have another baby—she's not too old. That actress just had a baby at forty-three. Like my father did, she could reject me and move on. I am being punished for the rest of my life. I try to do good things, but I just can't. It's safer if I never get up.

I hear someone coming up the stairs. It can't be Viv. It's not Tina—the steps are too heavy. It's Toad. He calls out my name. I don't answer. He knocks. "I'm coming in . . . whether you like it or not, so you better be decent." He pushes the door open.

I pull the sheet over me to cover my legs—I'm only wearing a T-shirt and underwear.

"It's like a tomb in here." Toad goes to the window and snaps the shade. Bright sunshine pours in.

"Ah!" I scream, and hide my face under the pillow. "What do you want, Toad?"

"You're not answering my calls. I want to see if you're still alive."

"Well, I am."

"It's so stuffy." He bangs on the window until he can get it open, and the breeze fills the room. "It's time to come out of your Hole."

"Why?"

"Because nothing happens in there. You'll waste away."

"Nothing happens out there either," I say.

"That's not true. For example, did you know it's seventy degrees today and everything is blooming?"

"Good for everything."

"Did you run this week?"

I shake my head.

"What happened to four times a week?"

"I'm on the honor system."

"Well, you're not being very honorable."

"I don't care."

"Tessa needs the exercise too, you know."

"She can run around the yard." I feel a pang of guilt. The yard is fine for Tessa, but it's not the same. She loves my runs more than anything.

"You have to take care of yourself," he says.

"You're not my mother," I say.

"This is true. Where is your mother, anyway?"

"She went away. We had a fight."

Toad shakes his head. "Why didn't you tell me? You could have stayed with me."

"You didn't want me," I remind him. "You're mad at me too."

"I'm not mad at you, Lopi. I just wish you wouldn't do things that hurt you. It's hard to see."

"Like what?"

"Like all this." He sweeps his arm around the room. I haven't kept it orderly for the last few weeks. There are clothes strewn about the floor and most surfaces. There are dirty coffee mugs and a bowl of half-eaten yogurt molding on the desk. I tried drawing and instead ripped up half my sketchbook, tossing the tattered paper everywhere. "This is not you," he says.

"It is now," I say.

Toad sits on my bed and puts his hand on my head. "Lopi. You need help."

I feel a well in my throat. I want to yell at him, push him away, tell him to mind his own business. I want to tell him that it's too late, that I am beyond help. "Just because my room is a mess?" I ask.

"No. You know what I mean. In general."

"Why do you care?" I mumble.

"I've known you too long not to," he says. He walks over to the bookshelf. "What's wrong with George the Twelfth?" he asks.

"What?" I sit up.

"He's just floating. I think he's dead."

"No." I get out of bed. "No, he was fine yesterday. He was fine." The fish is belly-up on the surface. I poke my finger in the bowl, but he doesn't move. "It was an accident," I say. The tears are streaming down my face. I start shaking.

"Hey, it's just a fish," Toad says. "Fish die all the time."

"You don't understand. I killed him."

Toad gives me a puzzled look.

"I killed him," I say again. "I didn't mean to, but I did."

Toad puts his arms around me and pulls me close. I bury my head in his long hair. He rubs my back and I wail into him, sobbing and shaking.

"Hey, hey," he says after a minute. "It's okay. It's just a fish. It's not that bad."

"No," I say. "I mean Adam. I killed my brother."

Adam

I recount to Toad what happened, how I remember it. How Adam left the car. How my father didn't look back. How there was a big thump and my father said, "What the hell did you kids leave in the driveway?"

I tell Toad how I disappeared in all the aftermath, standing on the side of the driveway when the ambulance came. It was no use, though; he had died instantly, they said. My mother let out a scream of terror and then went blank, and then started hitting my father screaming, "How could you? How could you?"

One of the ambulance people noticed me and said, "You might want to take her inside." My father carried me in, but it was too late: I had seen already. Adam's head unrecognizable, his skinny arm stretched straight over him, as if pointing at something. As soon as I got inside, I kicked off my new clogs and buried them deep at the bottom of the garbage.

Toad listens to me, not in horror as I expected, but with softness. He lets me say it all, then leans over and smoothes down my hair, as though he is petting a dog. As if on cue, Tessa comes into my room and nuzzles her head in my lap.

"I knew it was a bad accident," Toad says, "but I didn't know it was that bad. Why didn't you ever tell me?"

"I am an evil person," I say.

"You're not evil, Lopi! You were only six!"

"I could have stopped him."

"That doesn't make it your fault. I don't always stop my brothers from doing stupid things."

"But they didn't die."

"It was an accident, Lopi! A horrible, horrible accident. Besides, your parents should have strapped him in. What's wrong with them? If it's anyone's fault, it's theirs. And then for your mother to ignore you like she does . . ." He lets out an angry sigh.

I am surprised at how outraged Toad is.

"Is this what makes you so depressed all the time?" he asks.

"I don't know, maybe. Other things too, but mostly this."

"I really don't see how it's your fault. I mean, you loved Adam too. I remember you used to walk him down the driveway in his stroller and tell everyone he was your baby doll. He idolized you—he sat in there and pretended he was your doll."

Adam *was* very adoring. If only I could have done it all differently. If I could have made him stay in the car, told my parents he'd left, I'd be a different person. We would all be.

Sweeter Than Pie

Toad is being sweeter than pie. He comes over the next morning and walks to school with me, just to make sure I go. He even goes running with me, and I am surprised that he can keep up. Toad is more athletic than I remember him being. For some reason I have him stuck at about twelve years old, but he's not. He's turning into a man all of a sudden. And the thought of kissing him is becoming more and more appealing.

One day he comes over with a new fish. We clean out the bowl for George the Thirteenth.

"This is the lucky one," he says. "This one will last awhile."

I still don't know if George the Twelfth would have died as fast had I not exposed him to air, but I guess I'll never know. Just like I'll never know if Adam would have stayed in the car if I'd said anything.

"I brought Lucky George a new-home present." Toad takes a little plastic diver and a chest full of tiny gold coins out of a paper bag.

"That's cute," I say as I watch the diver float to the bottom of the bowl and hang out there. George the Thirteenth swims under its arm.

"His protector," Toad says.

"Thanks," I say, and am about to start crying.

"Hey, it's no big deal. It's just a cheap plastic diver. It only cost five dollars."

"No, I mean, for always being so nice to me. You've always been so nice to me."

"Well, I love you, Lopi." He says this like it means nothing, and in some ways it does mean nothing, because I know Toad loves me. But in another way, now all of a sudden it means everything.

I watch Toad as he absently picks at the plastic wrapping the diver came in.

"I love you too," I say. We smile at each other with a huge amount of tension, the good kind of tension, between us.

A Good Thing

It's been almost two weeks since Viv and I fought. Two weeks since Charley, who I've all but forgotten. Viv and I fall into a routine of avoiding each other, which is very easy to do, especially when she stays at Josh's every weekend. We pass any necessary information through Tina or notes on the refrigerator. It's okay because I think about Toad all the time now. He has always been my friend, he has always lived next door, but he has never been in my head so much as he is now. Could it be? The whole cliché of the boy next door seems so trite. I mean, come on—how could I not have noticed? But then I think of all the signs. I mean, he's been my best friend. What better person in the world to love? Is it possible that I could make a good choice for once in my life? And he keeps telling me that I am okay.

Friday evening, Viv is away and Toad comes over to go for a run. The moment I see him in his shorts and T-shirt I know that we will never be the same. I think he knows it too, because we hardly say anything to each other.

"Hi, Toad. Hi, Lopi." Tina greets us when we come in from running. "Hungry? I've got some stir-fry on the stove if you want it. I'll be out, so help yourself."

We barely acknowledge her and head upstairs.

"Hi," Toad whispers when we are alone in my room.

"Hi," I say.

Toad leans over and his mouth finds mine and we kiss and nothing feels more right in the whole world.

"I have wanted to do that for a long, long time," he says when we finally breathe.

"I know," I say. And then I add, "Me too." Even though I didn't realize it until just now. I kiss him again. "I've never had sex, you know," I say.

"I know," he says. "Me either."

"If you are my first that will link us forever. We'll never forget each other. We'll always be each other's first."

Toad smiles. "I don't mind."

I snuggle against him and sigh. "I don't mind either."

His body is firm and strong, not at all what I would have expected, but then, I knew him when he was a scrawny fifth-grader. He's not that anymore. We lie back on the bed and his weight is on me. I am surprised at how strangely normal it all seems, even the awkward parts, like how it takes a few tries to get the condom on, how we even laugh at our clumsiness. I am surprised that my life doesn't stop, that I am not transformed, that a few times I even think about mundane things, like did I remember to give Tessa fresh water and how good a hamburger would taste. I don't even mind that we both smell sweaty. In fact, I kind of like our smells together.

He is the same Toad, yet how different it is to see him so close up—to be able to trace the outline of his chin with my finger and kiss the freckles on his shoulder. And the best thing is that Toad does not disappear on me. It doesn't last long—after all, this is Toad's first time too. But it doesn't matter. After all the others, after my three strikeouts, this feels so right.

When we are done he spoons me and I ask, "So can you tell? Do I look non-virgin to you?"

"Hmm." He peers into my eyes, brushes the hair out of my face. "You look good," he says.

I curl under his arm as though I've always belonged there.

Toad leaves early in the morning, not wanting his parents to know he's been gone all night. I doze off and on, reliving the highlights of our night. I hear Tina get up, and smell fresh coffee brewing. I'm so happy I go downstairs to greet her.

"Hey there," she says. "What's up?"

"Oh, I don't know. Nothing really." I hop on one foot and then the other, not able to stand still.

She looks at me. "Really? You're grinning like a goofy gorilla, not to mention dancing like one too."

I laugh. "I'm in a good mood."

"That's nice for a change. It's been so quiet around here. I've been beginning to wonder who still lived here. I've hardly seen you or your mother for a couple of weeks. I thought maybe something was going on."

"Well, there is, was . . . well, we did fight, but even that can't cover my good mood." I stand there, wanting to blurt everything to Tina, but also wanting to keep Toad my secret, as if telling anyone would ruin it.

Tina studies me and then smiles herself. "You've still got that grin. What's going on?"

"I think I'm in love." There. I say it.

"That's great! That's a good feeling. Love." She sighs slightly. "Anyone I know?"

"Well, yeah, kind of."

"Not . . . "

I cut her off immediately. "No! This is someone real."

She waits. Tina is so much easier to share information with than Viv. She'd even be okay if I didn't tell her. Which makes me tell her. "It's my friend, Toad." Just saying his name makes me think of his freckly arms, his sweet kiss, his muscular legs. I know I am blushing. "I know I've known him forever," I say, "but this is different. I never really saw him before and now it's like I can see him."

Tina doesn't tease or question me, just nods. "Toad's a good guy."

"He is," I say.

Just then Viv and Josh storm in, each carrying a box of strawberries. "Look what's at the market! First of the season. Of course they're sent up from the south, but still." She sees me, and pauses. "What are you so happy about?"

All my good feeling falls like a rock right down to my toes. "Nothing." This time I mean it.

Tina glances from me to Viv.

Josh takes two strawberries from the box. "They're delicious. Have one."

Tina takes one and makes an *mmmm* noise.

I take the other, but don't eat it. "Thanks," I mumble. "I have homework to do." I turn around and head back upstairs.

"See what I'm talking about? She's such a pill these days," I hear Viv say. "She's been ignoring me for weeks, just because of a stupid dinner." I close my door before I hear anymore.

I lie on my bed and daydream of Toad, and slowly my smile returns.

Accident

At some point I know I'll have to talk to Viv, but I need a little more time. She's probably just obliviously enjoying her time with Josh, already planning to rent my room out.

School is kind of a joke these days, especially for seniors. They are all getting ready for the prom and graduation, so the last few weeks of classes hardly matter. Most everyone has heard from schools already. I got into State, big whoop, but haven't heard from the other one yet. I don't know what's taking them so long. Tina is insanely busy studying for finals, so she's hardly around either. It's like I live alone all of a sudden. It's actually nice to have it so quiet. And it's nice to think about Toad in such a new way. It's almost as if nothing else in the world matters except the two of us. We snuggle whenever we can find the place and the time and discover all sorts of new things about each other.

I think about myself in a slightly new way too. I think that maybe it is not all my fault about Adam, that it was an accident. That it is possible that I am not all evil. I don't know if Viv will see me that way, though.

After school I go out for my run, by myself this time. Toad has to work at Pizza Palace. I'm going to get a job there too, as soon as school is over. After the first mile I am coasting, the wind in my face, my legs carrying me swiftly, my feet barely touching the ground. I've heard that marathon runners go into a zone after the first few miles.

I think about Josh, Andrew, and Charley. They were all wrong for all the wrong reasons. Thankfully nothing happened with any of them. Thankfully it happened with Toad. For once I did something right. I will always love Toad, friend, neighbor, or lover. When I am an old woman I will remember him. I may even still know him. Who knows, he may even be an old man with me. It's not impossible. For now, it's kind of nice to think about.

Life is such a mix of good and evil. I think about Adam dying so young—he'd be twelve now. I think how my mother had to check out and never mention his name. I think about how I've managed to study so hard and get out of school. And then I go back to Toad. How can things be so good and so bad at the same time? I imagine what Elwood the Shrink might tell me. I think he might agree with Toad. I think he would forgive me. I keep running and let my thoughts just filter through my brain like you're supposed to do when you meditate. I manage an easy ten miles. Mr. Koch will be pleased.

After running I stretch for a long time, massaging my calf muscles. I check my phone. There are ten missed messages! As I am about to check who could possibly be calling so much, it rings. A restricted number.

"Hello?"

"Lopi! Where have you been? I've been trying to reach you!" Josh is practically hysterical. "There's been an accident."

"What?" I say, not registering his words.

"There was an accident. Vivian. We're in the hospital. They won't let me use the cell phone."

"What?" I ask again. "What?"

Josh takes a breath and speaks more clearly. "We were heading to the beach in the truck. Another truck came out of nowhere. It just hit us. I tried to swerve, but it came so fast."

Josh was driving. A truck hit them. They are in the hospital. I start to get it. A car accident. A goddamn car accident.

"Is she . . .?" I stop before I say *dead*. I can't ask that. It would be too, too awful. I can't live if she's dead. I'd be nothing.

"Lopi. It was bad. I don't know." He is wheezing into the phone.

"What about you?" I ask. I'm almost mad that he sounds okay. Why didn't he get hurt instead? Why Viv?

"I have some bruises. She wasn't wearing her seat belt. You know how she hates that. She was leaning over, she was leaning next to me. The truck hit her side."

Suddenly I am so pissed at her for being there in the hospital. She was probably leaning over to kiss him or play with his hair or whatever she does. Can't she wear a stupid seat belt?

"I have to hang up, but get here as soon as you can, okay?" The phone goes blank before I can answer.

I start running toward the hospital when I realize it will take too long. Even on my bike it would take too long. What if she dies before I get there? What if I don't ever get to talk to her again?

I call Toad. Voice mail. I leave a brief, semicoherent message—I don't want to come across as panicking. I don't really know how serious it is yet. "Toad, Viv was in an accident. I need a ride to the hospital. Call me back."

I try Tina—her phone is off. She must be in the library, or she could be home studying.

I call Apple. Voice mail. I hang up without leaving a message.

I even try Charley. I just need a ride. But I get his voice mail too. Where the hell is everyone?

I run home, hoping that Tina's car will be in the driveway. But when I get there, the only car is the Volvo, perched like a tombstone. I run inside and call Tina's name anyway. All is quiet. I open her door a crack just to be sure she's not studying with her headphones on, but she's not there and her book bag is gone.

I'll have to take the Volvo. There's no other choice. I find the keys on the kitchen shelf and I'm out the door. Before I know it I am sitting in the driver's seat. I go through the steps. Ignition on. Shift to R. Breathe. Check mirrors. Breathe. Release brake. Foot on gas. Breathe, breathe, breathe. Check mirror again. I back out slowly on to the street, shift to D, and go forward.

By the time I get to the hospital I realize I've hardly taken a breath and my knuckles are white from clutching the steering wheel, but I have made it with no panic attack. For a second I am triumphant—this is cause to celebrate—but then I remember that I am at the hospital and something has happened to my mother.

Why is it that in emergencies everything becomes disjointed? Actions are abrupt and mechanical, thoughts drift in random coherence, details are heightened, and you notice the oddest things. Everything is crisp as I walk down the hallway. An old woman with bird's-nest hair is in the hall, half sitting, half lying on a stretcher, a man in a tattered yellow bathrobe slowly walks his IV. The wheels rattle across the linoleum. The aide wears a hideous polyester blue and pink flower print vest, and I think how sad it is that she has to wear that. Metallic silver machines reflect under the fluorescent lighting. The tan-ness of the hallway carries a somber weight. There are no white angel nurses like my mother used to be.

There are sounds too: a whir, a hum, a beep, whispered voices hovering all around. Movement and sound is everywhere, yet at the same time everything is insanely still and quiet. The smell of medicine and antiseptic cleaner fills my nose.

I get to the front desk and manage to ask for Vivian Yeager.

"Are you a relative?" the nurse asks.

"She's my mother. I'm her daughter."

The nurse checks her computer. "I'm sorry, you'll have

to wait." She points to a row of chairs behind a glass door. "A doctor will be out soon."

Josh is there, sitting upright in a green plastic chair. He is haggard, his sandy curls all straggly, and there is a bruise on his cheek. When he sees me he jumps up and gives me a long hug. His face is cardboard.

We wait an eternity. Other people come and go, and everyone is tense, in pain, worried, as they wait for news about the person they came with. The room is thick with anxiety and fear.

Finally a doctor comes to us to explain. There was some internal bleeding. They were able to stop it, but she'll have to stay in the hospital a few days so they can keep an eye on her. We can go see her.

Death

I've never really thought my mother could die. I know I've wished she would disappear, that it would be easier if she weren't around, but I don't know if I knew what I was wishing. The thought of my mother resting in peace seems absurd. She has so much energy and life in her, it's impossible she could ever be still.

Adam died so purposelessly, in a split second of wrong moves. I had wished he would disappear and he did. I didn't stop him and I could have. One way to look at it is that I had made it happen; another way is that it happened.

Death is so final. I don't want my mother to die. I want her to run on the beach and holler in the wind, sing show tunes and dance with her friends. But I want my own life too.

When I see her in the hospital bed she is still. Peaceful even. Her eyes are closed. Her hair is back and there are some bandages on her cheek where she must have fallen against the window. She has an IV in her arm. She opens her eyes when we enter, and manages a smile. Josh rushes to her side and strokes her face.

I stand back a minute and then go over and take her hand, the one that is not attached to the IV. She squeezes it tight. Too tight.

My mother did not die. She is stable. She will be fine. She is alive.

Acceptance

Two days later, on the day that just so happens to be my seventeenth birthday, a thick envelope arrives in the mail. It is from the alternative college. Thick is good. I open it and sure enough it says they are delighted to accept me into their school and that I will be a strong asset to the community and so on. They include a semester schedule, housing information, another brochure, and say a bill will follow soon.

"I got in," I say to no one. Tessa comes over and licks my leg. I pat her. "It's my birthday and I got in," I say.

I should be thrilled.

That afternoon I visit Viv in the hospital for the third time in two days. They had to do surgery for the internal bleeding, but she is recovering well, already flirting with the doctors and nurses. We are being cordial to each other, both careful not to mention anything difficult. She apologizes for not being well enough to give me a proper

birthday. That's fine with me, really. She'll give me a present later. I don't tell her about the acceptance letter.

In the evening, Toad takes me out to dinner and gives me
a set of watercolors and a blank book. "For whatever," he
says. "I thought you might want to paint something."

"This is great!" I say. "Thank you." I lean across the
table and give him a kiss.

"I got into college," I say, when I lean back.

"Yeah," Toad says like he knew it already.

"I'm sorry I'm going to leave you here all alone. But it's
only a few hours away. We can visit. I'll have a dorm room
with my own bed." I wink at him.

"I'll visit," he says. "I'll be fine here. Really."

"I have a huge favor to ask you."

"What?"

"Do you want Tessa? I'm afraid Viv won't give her the
life she's used to."

Toad smiles. "I'd love to keep Tessa for you."

We kiss good night and get a little hot and heavy but
then stop ourselves. Sometimes kissing is enough.

Talk to Her

I am outside the door of Viv's hospital room. Yesterday she was eating normally, back to her chipper self, chatting up the nurses and on a first-name basis with everyone.

I am about to walk right in when I hear her and Josh talking in hushed tones. Josh says my name. I stand still in the hallway where they can't see me and strain my ears to listen.

"You've had a scare, Vivian, but you can't keep ignoring Lopi. That girl needs some help."

"She doesn't need me. She has it all figured out," Viv says.

"Don't you see her calls for attention?"

"She hates me. I try to talk to her and she just wants to be left alone."

"You need to try harder. Every child needs her mother. You only lost one child, not two."

My mother has no rebuttal to this. I think I hear her crying. I realize I have never heard my mother cry before. Not even after Adam.

"I love you, Vivian. You know that. I want to marry you. I'm waiting for your answer, and I'll wait as long as it takes. But you have got to acknowledge your daughter. You have got to make up with her."

"We used to get along. She used to do things with me. It's like she's become a different person."

"Maybe you did too. Talk to her."

"What did I do to deserve you? You're so good to me."

"Then marry me. You haven't given me an answer yet."

Viv sighs. "You won't love me forever. I'll get old on you."

"You know I don't care one iota about that, because I'll get old too."

"You'll always be younger, though."

"Yes, and I'll always love you. Promise me that you will talk to Lopi, that you will tell her you are here for her."

I don't hear my mother's answer. I think they are kissing. I tiptoe down the hall and wait for what I think is an appropriate amount of time, then enter.

Viv smiles when she sees me, wipes her eyes, and puts on her happy face.

"Hi, sweetie." She pats a spot on the bed for me to sit. She is propped up with pillows and wearing her white nightgown with the red cherries on it that Josh gave her for her birthday. Josh is standing on the bedside near the window, holding her hand. There are flowers and cards all around.

"So, tell me, how you've been? What's new in school?

Are you still going to graduate this year?" she asks, trying to be all bubbly.

"Yes," I say. "I'm doing fine. I'm pretty sure I have an A in English and A's and B's in most everything else. Looks like Mr. Koch is okay with my running reports."

"You're so together, so smart. Isn't she smart, Josh?" Josh nods. Viv goes on. "Wise, really. You know what to do to get what you want. I was never that wise when I was your age. I made so many mistakes."

"I'm going to go get a sandwich in the cafeteria," Josh says. I know he's trying to give us some alone time. "Are you two all set here? Do you need anything?"

I shake my head, but Viv says, "Could you be a darling and get me a coffee milk shake? They only serve regular ice cream up here, and I want something thick and creamy that I can sip through a straw."

"You got it." He bends over and kisses her cheek.

"You are a doll. Love you."

"You, too." He shuts the door behind him and we are alone.

I watch out the window as the clouds wisp in the wind.

Viv follows my gaze. "Looks beautiful out there."

"It is."

There's an awkward silence.

"I'll be coming home tomorrow," Viv finally says. "It's nice to be waited on, but I can't wait to get home. I'm so tired. A hospital is no place to rest—they come in all night long, checking this, poking that, noises going off, everything bleeping."

"I'm sorry," I say.

"Nothing you can do, honey. I'm just looking forward to my own bed."

"No. I'm sorry I got so mad at you. I didn't mean those things I said when Charley was over. I don't hate you."

Viv takes my hand and holds it in hers. "I know that. At least, I think I know that. Though sometimes it seems as though you don't like me very much."

"I don't like how you try to run my life and then ignore me."

"You act as though you want to be left alone all the time," she says defensively.

I can feel this starting to turn into an argument and I try to stop it. "Everything changed," I say.

The corners of Viv's cheeks flinch and her grip tightens slightly, but she doesn't say anything. I want to tell her when and why everything changed. I want to tell her why I did what I did, but I don't know if I can explain it or if she'll be as understanding as Toad. Can she ever forgive me? I don't know if I can ever fully forgive myself.

Josh comes back with the milk shake and puts it on the side table, then says he's going for a walk.

"Are you still seeing Charley?" Viv asks when he leaves. Suddenly I realize this is as hard for her as it is for me. She doesn't know how to talk about it either. Any other topic is easier. I shake my head no.

"That's too bad," she says. She takes a sip of her milk shake. "Oh, this is perfect, delicious. Want some?" She holds out the Styrofoam cup. I shake my head no again.

We sit another minute. I think about telling her about

Toad, but I'll wait. There's no hurry. She likes Toad fine, but I know she'll tease me and I don't want that. Besides, there are more important things to tell her.

"Mom," I say, and she raises her brows, startled. I never call her that. "It's my fault."

"No, shhh. Honey. Nothing is your fault."

"But it is."

"No, honey. Don't say anything. You don't have to say anything."

"But that's just it. I should have said something!"

"What are you talking about, honey?"

"Adam," I say his name. I can't look at her, but I keep talking. "I couldn't get him strapped in. I saw him leave the car. I didn't stop him. I'm the reason he . . ."

"What?" Viv says, firmly enough for me to look up. Her face contorts and her mouth opens, letting out quick breaths.

I shake my head. "I'm the reason he's dead. And I'm probably the reason Dad left too. I wanted it to be just you and me."

She opens her mouth and starts to say something, but I turn away. I back toward the door. I hear her say my name, but I ignore her. I run into the hallway and down the emergency stairs, out the sliding-glass exit of the hospital and into the street, where the fresh air slaps my face. I am running and crying. I'm always running. Running nowhere.

"Lopi! Lopi!" Josh is running after me. He was in the park across from the hospital. He reaches me and I stop. "What happened?" he asks. "Where are you going?"

"You wouldn't understand." I stare at the sidewalk.

"I understand more than you think. You and Vivian are more alike than you might know. You're both stubborn and you both blame yourselves."

I tilt my head. What does he know?

"She thinks you hate her," he says.

"But I want her to be happy," I say. To myself I think that he is right, that sometimes I do hate her.

"She might never be able to be happy, but she can be happier. I think she is happier with me. You know that I love her."

"I know." I kick a pebble with the toe of my shoe. It flips in the air and lands on the pavement between us.

"And you know that she loves you," Josh says.

"She has a funny way of showing it."

"Go back and talk to her," he says. "Don't let her change the subject. She's like a little kid that way. Don't let her get away with that."

It strikes me that he is right. It is as if she is younger than both of us. Maybe she'll never get over Adam, maybe the only way she can deal is by not dealing, maybe she will never forgive me, but I have to find out. What I did was wrong, but it was an accident. A tragic accident. If it had gone another way, maybe nothing would have happened. Even if I had said something Adam might have left anyway, but that didn't necessarily mean I was evil. Right?

I go back in and find Viv with a pile of tissues strewn all over the bed.

"You're back," she says, quickly trying to cover the tissues with the blanket.

"You're crying," I say.

"Caught me!" She smiles and makes light of it. "You shouldn't have to see your old mother such a wreck."

"You're not old," I say.

She sighs. "I am getting older. I feel older."

"Well, maybe that's not a bad thing."

"You're going to be gone soon, Lopi, and I won't have you around anymore. I don't know if I can bear losing you."

"I'm just going to college. I'm not dying."

We both stop short.

"About Adam," I start.

Viv puts her hand up. "That's the past, Lopi. It's in the past."

"But I want to talk about it. We never talk about him. Did you hear what I said before?"

Viv stretches out her arms and I walk closer to her. "You were six years old," she says. "You were practically a baby yourself. And me too. I never should have married so young. Having a baby at twenty-four. Your father was so handsome, so persuasive. I thought he was it." She pauses, then goes on. "Your dad backed up . . . I thought he had put him in his seat, he thought I had. You weren't responsible." She holds my shoulders and peers straight into my eyes. "Whatever you did or did not do, whatever you thought, it is not your fault." We are both crying. "I want to hear you say it. Tell me it is *not* your fault."

And I do. I say it. "It's not my fault." I wail into her.

The nurse comes in to check on all the commotion, but Viv waves her out.

"There, there, sweetie. My honey. It's okay." She rubs my back. "It was an accident," she whispers.

We hug and cry for a while and then Viv wipes her eyes. "Let's start new, sweetie. I am happier now. Josh asked me to marry him. I'm going to say yes."

I give a teary nod.

"I think you should start seeing a therapist. A good one, someone to talk to who can help you figure all this stuff out. Someone who can help you to forgive yourself. How would you feel about that?"

"Can we afford it?" I ask.

"We'll have to."

"I'll get a job soon. And when I get to college there'll be someone at the health services, I bet, and that would be covered in my tuition," I say.

"We'll find someone for you this summer until then."

"Okay." Far be it for me to argue. No more talking to Elwood in my head. I think maybe my mother and I can actually start new, but I'm not going to give up the chance to see a shrink finally. Even having Toad around now, I know I could use some professional help.

"By the way," I say. "I got in to the college I wanted."

Viv pats my hand. "Of course you did." She takes a breath and then she says something I never thought she'd say. "I know I haven't been the best mother for you. I checked out. I'm sorry, honey. Can you ever forgive me?"

I nod. Maybe I can.

A Good Cleaning

It's so quiet when I get home. The house practically echoes, and this time I don't like it. I actually miss Viv's hustle and bustle and bursts of energy. Even Tessa wanders around aimlessly. Tina is almost done with school—her graduation is in a week. Mine is in three. Tina has decided to stay the summer and then move to Boston in the fall.

Viv is coming home tomorrow.

Tina has made a big pot of soup, but I am not hungry. I pace the house, restless for something to do. I can't read or study. I can't sleep either. I pull out all the cleaning supplies from under the sink and line them up on the kitchen counter. First I organize them and then I start to use them. I dust every knickknack, every corner. I dust the leaves on the plants. I clean the ashes from the fireplace. I get a bucket of soapy water and wash the outside and the inside of the oven, grabbing up globs of grime that have probably been there for ten years.

At some point Tina comes in and says it looks like I'm getting ready for a party. This gives me an idea.

I call Toad. "You know that party I was going to have?"

"Oh, no. Don't tell me you're going to have it now, while your mom's in the hospital."

"No, better. She's coming home tomorrow and I thought I'd have a surprise party for her. You know, a welcome-home thing, just a couple friends. Do you think she'd like it?"

"Your mom? She'll be ecstatic."

I call Josh and tell him my idea. He thinks it's great and makes a couple calls. We get Tina in on it and she starts preparing food.

Toad comes over and helps clean. He's mopping the kitchen floor while I'm in the upstairs bathroom, scrubbing the toilet. As I am cleaning I realize I am looking forward to Viv coming home.

I hear Toad come up the stairs. "Are you done mopping already?" I say. "Good—I could use you to scrub the shower stall."

"Only if you'll join me in it—naked."

I turn around. He's leaning against the doorway and I immediately want to jump his bones.

"Hi, gorgeous," he says.

"Yeah, right." My unwashed hair is pulled back with a dirty scarf, I'm wearing my rattiest sweats, and I am covered in grime.

Toad leans next to me and takes the toilet brush out of my hand. "You're sweet," he says, and his lips find mine.

"Thanks," I say after a minute of kissing. "But I've got

to finish here. Are you going to help or are you going to distract me?" I shove a sponge at him and he wrings it out and goes to work. Every once in a while I look over at his sexy body scrubbing the dirty shower and smile.

Homecoming

Viv's friends show up just after noon. Tina has made mini cucumber and avocado sandwiches, pickled beets, potato salad with rosemary, and fresh-squeezed lemonade. The house sparkles. There are fresh flowers on the table. It all looks lovely.

Sandra and Kenneth are there, and Viv's yoga instructor. Tina, of course, and Toad. I even invite Charley and Apple. They are going out now, which makes perfect sense. I bet Apple has already taught Charley a thing or two. I'm glad we can all still be friends.

Josh leaves to go pick up Viv.

I step back and look at all of us. This is my party for my mother. I can't wait for her to see the place so clean. In a way it's like this is my graduation party too. I feel as though I am already beginning something new. Toad walks over to me, takes my hand, and squeezes it gently. We wait for the Volvo to drive up.